OUT IN THE OFFENSE

LANE HAYES

For Zack- Sports may not be your thing, but you tried it all and found your own voice along the way. I'm so proud of the fierce LGBTQ warrior you've become. Thank you for taking us with you on your journey. I learn more from you everyday than you'll ever know.

1

"You cannot teach a man anything; you can only help him find it within himself."—Galileo

THE LATE AFTERNOON sun glinted off the bleachers and sent a prism of light across the Astroturf. The ultra-green hue gleamed even brighter than usual at this time of day and contrasted nicely with the longer shadows. It might be eighty degrees in the shade still, but fall was definitely coming. We were a few weeks into the new school semester and three games into our football season. Thankfully, we'd won by respectable margins. A minor miracle, considering a slew of our better players graduated last spring. Starting over with a mostly unseasoned crew wasn't optimal, but so far, things were looking good.

Which usually meant bad news was on the horizon.

Hey, I wasn't a downer. If anything, I considered myself a realist. Nothing good lasted forever—including winning streaks. I signaled a play to Gonzalez, one of the faster running backs on our team, then pulled my arm back and launched the football into the air in a high, tight spiral. It sailed in a perfect arc for sixty yards and hit my target right in his hands. Gonzalez secured the ball and ran like the wind toward the end zone.

I laughed when he let out a loud whoop and broke into a ridiculous victory dance. A few of the other guys joined in, but the second our head coach, Flannigan, blew his whistle, everyone hustled off the field. I waved absently to a couple of the assistant coaches chatting on the sideline as I jogged toward the locker room and then groaned when Coach Perez stepped aside and motioned me over.

Mike Perez was our offensive coordinator and an all-around good guy. But the dude could talk, and it had already been a long day. The last thing I wanted to do was go over additional plays. Surely it could wait until morning.

"Yo, Rafferty!"

I veered left to meet him and pulled off my helmet. "What's up, Coach?"

Perez was a husky man in his late thirties with jet-black hair and a receding hairline he hid with a ubiquitous baseball cap. He was about five inches shorter than my six four with a completely different build. He looked more like a linebacker now than a former quarterback, but twenty years ago, he'd played my position at a private college similar to Chilton. He knew the ins and outs of a Division-Three program at a school better known for academics than athletics. I respected his football acumen, but I liked him as a person too. He was quick to laugh and had a habit of talking about his wife and kids that was kind of endearing. I thought it was cool that as much as he loved the game, his family always came first.

"That arm's looking good, man. How are you feeling?" he asked, adjusting the rim of his cap.

"Great." I squinted and gave him a funny look. "Don't tell me you're adding a complicated play I need to perfect in two days."

"Nah." He nodded at a couple of guys passing by and then inched closer to me in a maneuver that clearly indicated this was a private conversation. "I like what we've got down."

"Oookay…" I wracked my brain, wondering what I'd done wrong while I waited for him to continue. Practice went well today. My arm was strong, my decision-making was on point, my feet were sure and—

"Your academic advisor called today. Mrs. Landau."

"Oh." *Fuck.*

He tilted his head in what could only be described as a "concerned parental" look before continuing in a lower tone. "She said you're failing statistics. She also mentioned this is the second time you've taken the course and because you're a senior, it's your last chance to pass if you're gonna graduate on time. Apparently, she's contacted you about tutoring but you either haven't acted on it, or you've ignored her messages entirely. Why?"

I let out a frustrated huff and pushed my hand through my hair. "It's the middle of September. There's plenty of time to—"

"To do the right thing," he intercepted. "It's a two-part course. You can't afford to fail, man. One of the perks of being a student athlete is having immediate access to first-rate tutoring. You have to sign up, Rafferty."

I frowned but nodded my acquiescence. "Okay. I will."

"Good. I need proof it's done before I put you in the game Saturday."

"Wait. What?" I pulled at the sleeve of his burgundy polo shirt and tried to ignore my suddenly accelerated heartbeat.

Coach glanced down at his sleeve until I released my hold, then glowered at me. "What's the problem? I'm covering my ass while you do yourself a favor and get the help you need. It's a win-win, see?"

"Right," I replied automatically.

I scratched the back of my neck and grimaced. *Fuck.* I knew it. Wasn't I just thinking something would blow up any second? There had to be a way around this. Maybe I knew someone who could help me. One of the guys on the team might know statistics. I did a mental roll call of my teammates while my coach fixed me with a laser-beam, no-bullshit gaze.

"You gotta level with me, man. If you're not gonna follow through, there will be consequences and frankly, this team can't afford to have their star quarterback on the bench. This is a small school. If you actually do fail, word will get out and this program will be under fire for not stepping in to help. It's not just about you. Our reputations are on the line too. What's the problem here, Christian?"

I did a double take when he used my first name. I wasn't sure he remembered I had one. I swallowed hard. No doubt this would sound stupid to anyone besides my sister, but I had to tell him something, because sitting out even one game wasn't going to happen.

I shrugged and pursed my lips. "I know it sounds crazy but... my parents will flip. My dad works for the administration. If I sign up for on-campus tutoring, he'll find out about it, and I can't deal with people being disappointed in me for a subject I don't give a fuck about when what really matters is the game."

"Wrong. What really matters is getting an education and living a good life. Hey, I love this sport as much as you do. I get it. But unless you plan on coming back for a fifth year, you're nearing the end of your tenure here. If you want to stay on, I can tell Mrs. Landau you'll drop the second part if you don't pass and—"

"I can't stay another year. I have to graduate," I said.

"Then get a damn tutor. Geez, I'd think your folks would be proud of you for asking for help when you need it," he huffed.

"Yeah well, they're not those kinds of parents. The last thing

I need is to have my father micromanaging my schedule any more than he already does, but..." I paused when my brain started cranking out ideas. A few of which didn't totally suck. "What if I found someone unaffiliated with Chilton to tutor me? Would that work?"

He nodded slowly. "I don't see why not. Did you have someone in mind?"

"No. But I'll work on it and get back to you tomorrow. Is that cool?"

"Sure, but—Rory!" Perez snapped his fingers and grinned, clearly pleased with himself.

"Who's Rory?"

"He's an after-school camp counselor at the Y. My kids love him. He just graduated last May from Long Beach State. I don't think he's found a full-time job yet, but I do know he's a math whiz. You wouldn't know it by looking at him," Coach said with a laugh. "Rory was on the wrestling team in college. He reminds me of one of our linebackers. Until he starts talking about geometry."

"Why doesn't he have a job then? It's a decent economy. Seems weird that he wouldn't have found anything," I commented. I hated that I sounded like my dad, but unfortunately I'd inherited his relentless quest to be well-versed in details. No matter how inconsequential they seemed.

"He's a bit of a wild card, but he's a good soul and a smart motherfucker too. He told me he made extra cash in college from tutoring. I bet he'd help. I'll talk to him tonight when I pick up my kids. If he says he has time to take you on and his rate is reasonable, I'll have him call you. Sound good?"

"Sure. Thank you," I replied with a tight smile.

Coach clasped my shoulder and then headed off the field.

I stood alone for a moment, willing myself not to be overwhelmed by the instant wave of anxiety. A tutor? Fuck, that sounded awful. Like a total and complete pain in the ass. But I couldn't afford to fail. I had to play at the top of my game...and graduate on time.

⸻

MOST COLLEGE CAMPUSES had the same chill-yet-eager vibe, regardless of their size. And Long Beach State was fucking huge. I glanced at the map I'd pulled up on my phone and then at my surroundings. Students bustled with varying degrees of urgency, crossing the grassy quad area or walking along the tree-lined pathways to their classes. I supposed I could stop someone to ask for directions, but a giant blue pyramid-shaped gymnasium shouldn't be too hard to find.

I'd agreed to meet Rory Kirkland at his alma mater the following Monday afternoon before practice. Perez set the whole thing up. He'd suggested asking Rory to come to Orange or to meet halfway, but I insisted it was perfectly convenient for me to make the twenty-minute trip after my dreaded statistics class. It wasn't. Traffic was sluggish on the way there, and it would certainly be worse on the return drive. But a quirky part of me I couldn't easily explain wasn't ready to invite a stranger into my space. I'd rather observe the guy in his own environment and get a feel for him without my well-meaning coach inserting himself into the middle of an awkward meeting. It was probably a warped effort to exert control over something that left me feeling powerless. Passive-aggressiveness at its finest.

I took a right at a giant fountain and quickened my pace when I spotted the modern-style building at the end of the path. I hiked my backpack on my right shoulder and glanced around the park-like expanse of grass in front of the gym before taking a seat on the edge of a stone bench. I ignored the gaggle of peppy young girls on the other end and pulled out my cell to let Rory know I'd arrived and where to find me. I also added that I had a red backpack, thinking it would make it easier to spot me in the crowd. He responded immediately with a thumbs-up sign.

Great. I sat up straight and cast my gaze toward the entrance. This was definitely not your average gym. I loved the contemporary design. It was eye-catching but tasteful, I mused as a few volleyball players stepped outside, tossing a ball between them. Three of the men were taller than me with long, lanky physiques, but the fourth was much smaller. If he hadn't been wearing the same jersey as the others, I wouldn't have thought he was on their team. He laughed at something one of his friends said before turning around to greet a tattooed hottie who came through the door behind him. I looked down at my phone, then up again just as Mr. Tattoo snaked his arm around the volleyball player, pulled him close, and kissed him. In broad daylight.

I lowered my sunglasses and stared for a moment before glancing around the quad to see if anyone else noticed or gave a shit. I knew it was ridiculous, but old habits died hard. I grew up in an extremely conservative household. No joke—my folks went apeshit crazy when they heard that one of our top players had come out by kissing his boyfriend at a major end-of-season game last year. They'd asked me a million accusatory questions like they thought I was in on it. Honestly, I was as shocked as everyone else. I hadn't known Evan was bi or seeing someone. But I loved the guy like a brother, and I was happy for him. I smiled at the memory of Evan coming out to our team, then refocused on the tatted hunk.

He was standing on his own now, peering at his watch. Damn, he was sexy. Tall and toned with golden skin and—I winced when my cock swelled against my zipper. *Oh, fuck.* I yanked my sunglasses off and scrolled unseeing through my phone until I had my breathing under control again. The last thing I needed was to meet my new tutor sporting a hard-on. Where was he anyway? He should have—

"Hey, are you Christian?"

I shaded my eyes as I looked up and—*no way*.

I licked my lips nervously and stood. "Uh...yeah. You're Rory?"

"Yeah," he said in a low, deep voice that sent a tingle of awareness along my spine.

The corner of his mouth lifted in a roguish twist I supposed doubled as a smile. On anyone else, it might have come across as a poor imitation with an insulting lack of sincerity. On Rory, it was kind of badass. He exuded a James Dean cool with panache. I was a couple of inches taller than him. I knew I stood out among the jocks at Chilton, but I felt small next to Rory. And ordinary. I had brown hair, blue eyes, and maybe I was considered attractive, but he was...*wow*.

He had a thick build, short dark-blond hair, brilliant blue eyes, and a chiseled jaw and cheekbones. He wasn't classically handsome, but he was striking. His sheer size alone probably turned heads. Those muscles were a thing of beauty. I couldn't help noticing the way his thick biceps and broad shoulders tested the fabric of the sleeves on his black T-shirt. And that ink...damn. The swirling colorful design had nautical and fiery elements that made me curious about what was underneath his clothes.

Gulp. I clandestinely adjusted my backpack to cover my crotch and extended my right hand in greeting. He glanced from my outstretched hand to my mouth and back again before sliding his palm against mine and fuck...I almost came in my jeans.

Okay, here's the thing...I knew I was gay. I'd known it for years. At least since I was twelve. But the closet door was closed, and the lock was temporarily secure. I'd become an expert at playing it cool and acting unfazed by guys I found attractive. But Rory wasn't my type. I didn't go for muscular guys who looked like they could kick my ass. So why was I suddenly sweating? It had to be because I'd just seen him stick his tongue down his boyfriend's throat. I hadn't expected him to be gay...and sexy as fuck. This could be bad. Real bad.

I fumbled for my sunglasses and cleared my throat. "Nice to meet you. Uh...so you're the statistics guru?"

He raised a single brow and flashed another slow grin. "I prefer the term 'mad math genius.' "

I chuckled. "All right..."

"Did you bring your book?" he asked with a smile.

I tapped the side of my bag and nodded. "Yep. I have about an hour before I have to get back on the road. I figured you could look over the book and make sure you're interested before we discuss money."

"Sounds fair."

"Um...cool. So should we do this here or..." I paused when a figure behind us waved and called out something I couldn't quite hear over the chattering girls on the opposite side of the bench. "Hey, I think your boyfriend is trying to get your attention."

Rory glanced over his shoulder and returned the gesture before turning to face me with an unreadable expression. Not quite defensive, but definitely guarded. "What makes you think he's my boyfriend?"

"I saw you together and um, you know..."

"Ahh. So you were spying on me?"

"No! No, I was just sitting right here and I—"

"Dude, I'm kidding." Rory snickered. "You can take a picture if you want. It's cool by me. But for the record, James isn't my boyfriend."

"He's just a guy you kiss," I said in a flippant attempt to strike the right amount of nonchalance.

"Sometimes," he replied evasively.

"Right. Where should we go?"

He stared at me for a long moment, then hooked his thumb toward the path I'd come down. "The library is close enough. Let's head over there. You can tell me about yourself on the way. Perez said you're a quarterback. Is that right, or was he tryin' to impress me?"

"Yeah, but I wouldn't be too impressed. Chilton is a D-Three program. We draw the local crowds and play other private colleges but—"

"I know how college sports work, man. Don't undersell yourself. You must be a decent athlete. Perez was practically drawin' hearts and fuckin' flowers when he was talking about you."

I snorted in amusement. "Fucking flowers? That sounds nasty."

Rory stopped in his tracks and grinned. This time his eyes lit from within, transforming the cocky lift of his lips into something almost boyish. The contrast of his playful expression with his gorgeous tats did something to me. My stomach flipped and my palms were slick again. *Not good.*

"Someone's got a kinky side," he singsonged.

I pointed at my chest and shook my head. "Me? No, not me," I lied.

Rory shot a dubious glance my way, then gestured toward an empty bench tucked under a pepper tree. "Let's just sit here."

"I thought you wanted to go to the library."

"Yeah, but this is quiet enough. We aren't going to have time to get too in-depth anyway. And you look a little unsure about me. I wanna give you a clear path to the parking lot in case you decide I'm a psycho."

I started to argue even though I knew he was kidding. I caught myself and asked, "Are you?"

He waggled his brows and grinned mischievously. "Absolutely. But I'm the harmless kind."

"Aren't we all?" I replied glibly as I followed him to the bench.

It was set back a foot or so from the walkway, giving the space an illusion of privacy. I sat on the end and dropped my backpack in the middle. Any distance was welcome at this point —my nerves were on edge. I pulled my textbook out and set it on the canvas bag between us.

He picked up the book and idly thumbed through the pages. "Where're you from?"

"Uh...why?" I asked with a frowning.

Rory rolled his eyes. "We're getting to know each other, remember? If *you're* the psycho, I oughtta know about it."

I snickered. "You're safe with me. I'm not too crazy."

"That's what they all say," he snarked. "So...keep talkin'."

"I live in Orange, about ten minutes from school."

"Roommates?"

"Two. Max and Sky. They both play baseball."

"Hey, that's a coincidence. Those are my dogs' names!"

"Really?"

"No. I don't have a dog," he deadpanned. Then he winked and gave me another show-stopping ear-to-ear grin, adding, "But when I do, I'll name him Max."

I lowered my sunglasses and hooked them on the collar of my T-shirt. "You're weird. And I think you're the one who's supposed to be doing the talking and wowing me with your big brain."

"Yeah, but you won't remember anything if you're nervous."

"What makes you think I'm nervous?" I bluffed.

Rory made a funny face and gestured toward my fidgety hands. "You can't sit still."

I unzipped my backpack and gave him a lopsided smile. "I can't help it. Math makes me jumpy. I can conjugate the hell out of a verb, but numbers make no sense to me. It's even worse when math tries to disguise itself with words. I have a recurring nightmare of sitting alone in a locked classroom with a page full of word problems. It gets darker and darker in the room, and somehow I know I won't be released until I can figure out the answers."

"Damn, that sounds scary," he commented with a low whistle.

"It is! And statistics is nothing more than a series of endless word problems."

"Not really. It's about concepts." He shifted on the bench, bending his knee as he faced me with an almost manic look of excitement. "And life is a series of concepts rationed by levels of probability."

I fixed him with a blank stare, then blinked madly as my brain tried to compute how someone who looked so fierce could sound like such a geek. Better question—why did that turn me on?

"Like I said, I don't get it."

"I guarantee you understand more than you give yourself credit for." He raised his hand before I could disagree. "Think of it this way. In any given situation, there can be a multitude of outcomes. A, B, C, etcetera. Take me for example. I got out of school four months ago. I have a few options. I could A, get a so-called real job with real benefits or B, tutor math and coach wrestling. There's always C...I could continue working as an escort and—"

"You're an escort?"

Rory held my gaze for a second, then threw his head back

and laughed like a loon. "No, I just wanted to make sure I had your attention. Look, it's simple. Statistics is all about finding probability. However, you have to research the subject before you can make an educated guess."

"So you're saying I should get to know you to see if you'd make a decent escort?"

"It would help," he commented with a sly wink. "For the record, I'd suck at it. I have zero patience, and I hate being told what to wear or how to act. I think my tolerance level for all things bullshit is lowering with age."

"How old are you?" I interrupted.

"Twenty-four. Didn't we go over that?"

"No. I don't even know where you're from. I don't know anything about you except that you're an after-school counselor at the Y and that you used to wrestle in college."

He let out a beleaguered sigh and gave me a sideways once-over. "I'm from Long Beach. I've lived in the LBC my whole life. I had grand plans to go out of state for college, but the scholarship I was counting on didn't include room and board, so I came here. I graduated last May, top of my class, if that matters to you. And now I'm on a job hunt. I do the counselor thing, and I'm a trainer. I've thought about expanding my client list 'cause the money is decent, but I could probably do better if I used my degree. I have résumés out and I've even gone on a few interviews, but I haven't found anything yet."

"You will," I assured him. "Or maybe you should get your master's degree first."

"Thanks, Dad. I'll think about it."

I gave a half laugh. "Sorry. I sound like my father. He's nagging me to go to law school after I graduate."

"If that's your passion, go for it. Rack up all those degrees, frame 'em, and hang 'em on a wall. Grad school costs money, though, and baby...I'm broke," he huffed.

"You could apply for grants and scholarships," I suggested.

"Sure, but I'd rather work and if possible, not take on any debt." He regarded me thoughtfully, then inclined his head. "So you're going to be a lawyer, eh? Law school is—"

"I'm not going to law school," I intercepted vehemently.

Rory's gaze sharpened. "What do you want to do?"

The urge to confide in someone besides Max was strong. But I didn't know Rory, and I was too superstitious to share my plans with a stranger and upset my karmic shot at a new start. I looked away for a moment, then turned back to him with a blank expression.

"I don't know," I said. "I just know I'm not going to law school."

His eagle-eyed look flustered me. He didn't prod, though. He nodded in silent understanding and flattened his hand over the textbook.

"Well, maybe statistics can help."

"I doubt it, but as long as I pass and graduate on time, I'll consider it a win."

He let out a half laugh and pursed his lips. "Fair enough. I can help. We can get down and dirty next time, but like I said, I bet you know more than you think you do. Quarterbacks use statistics all the time."

"How do you figure?"

"Every time you decide who to throw the ball to in a clutch play, you use experience and data to analyze the field before you act. It's math."

"That seems like a stretch."

Rory shrugged. "It's not, grasshopper. And I'm the genius here. Not you."

I barked a quick laugh and cocked my head. I liked him. His sense of humor had a gentle bite he balanced nicely with a dose of self-deprecation. His looks, size, and unexpectedly big brain were intimidating and yet, there was something approachable and honest about Rory that made me think he'd be personally invested in my success if he was my tutor.

"All right, genius. Let's do this. How much do you charge? How often can you meet? What's your schedule like?"

"Perez is paying me. Don't ask me why. Ask him. We can meet once or twice a week. My schedule is all over the map, but I can work around your classes and practices. Any other questions?"

Yes. About a million. They ranged from practical to down-right nosy. I should ask about finding a good in-between place to meet and his preferred contact method. And grill him for info about why my coach offered to pay my bill. But I was more curious about the intricate design on his left bicep and the size of his muscular thighs. His nearness excited me. Truthfully, I didn't care what we talked about. I just didn't want to leave until I knew a little more about him.

So I opened my mouth, inserted my foot, and blurted, "Are you gay?"

Rory's automatic frown turned into a slow-moving devilish smile completely void of warmth. He didn't exactly look pissed, but he didn't look friendly either.

"Does it matter?" he countered.

"Of course not. I mean…I don't know why I asked. I guess I was curious about the volleyball player. You don't look gay." I winced and waved my hands as though the gesture might erase my stupidity. "I didn't mean that. I…I'm sorry. It's not my business."

"No, it's not." Rory leaned back in an ultracasual pose that contrasted sharply with the tension radiating from him. "Are you?"

"Me?" Heat flooded my cheeks and sent internal sirens screeching inside of me. My hands were sweating, my heart raced, and I was sure he could hear my brain rattle against my skull when I shook my head. "I'm too busy for relationships. I'm just focusing on my future. I'm—no."

He narrowed his eyes and nodded slowly.

"Yeah, I get it. I used to say that too." He held up his hand to stop my speech when I sputtered indignantly. "Save it. I don't need the apology. No, it's not your business who I fuck unless I'm fucking you, but since you asked so...nervously...I'm bi, with a strong preference for dick. If you are too, cool. If not, also okay. But if you've got a problem with me, speak up now. I don't want to waste my time or Perez's money."

I swallowed hard and held eye contact for as long as possible before opening my textbook. I pointed at the first thing on the page that looked like hieroglyphics to me. "What do you know about axioms of probability?"

Rory regarded me thoughtfully, then leaned back again and straightened his long legs in front of him. "A lot. There are three axioms..."

His lips were moving but I couldn't understand a thing he said anymore. The phenomenon was consistent for me. The hint of mathematic lingo sent me into an insta-coma-like state. But I wasn't in a hurry to get away or drown him out with my own inner soundtrack.

I might not be interested in the subject matter, but my tutor definitely had my attention. I admired Rory's unpolished and unapologetic style. And I was more than a little fascinated that under his cool dude exterior, he was a garden-variety math geek. Call me crazy, but maybe this tutoring thing wouldn't be so bad after all.

THE STUDENTS, faculty, and alumni of Chilton took their football seriously. And as quarterback and team captain, I was the team's representative and to some degree, a school ambassador. I usually worked out at the facility next to the football field, where the state-of-the-art equipment was always clean. But it was impossible to get a decent sweat on without stopping to chat with random people about how the team was doing and if I thought we'd crush the opposition at next week's game.

It had taken me a couple of years to grow into my role. But after three seasons as starting quarterback, I'd learned how to keep the sports enthusiasts happy without giving myself away. And I'd done a damn good job of it, if I said so myself. Sometimes that meant avoiding on-campus facilities and working out at the local gym down the street from my apartment. Midafternoons tended to be less crowded there, which made it an ideal place to lift weights and have a mini therapy session. Even if my faux therapist was my ex.

I couldn't decide if it was a blessing or a curse that the only person on the planet who knew the real me was Max. Actually, that wasn't true. Max and I were better friends than lovers. He was wildly unpredictable, but I trusted him. And I had to talk to someone about Rory, because a few days after meeting with him, I couldn't stop thinking about my new tutor. Rory had a snarky sense of humor and unapologetic self-confidence. He seemed to have a million sharp edges, but I could tell he had a softer side too. Add in a hunky physique and it was no wonder he'd unwittingly starred in a couple of my nightly jack-off sessions this week.

I shivered slightly at the fantasy I'd conjured last night. We were in a library behind a huge stack of books. One second Rory was pointing out an important detail on a page and the next, his hands were all over me. He pulled at my shirt, unbuckled my belt, unbuttoned and unzipped my Levis, then roughly turned me to face the shelves with a strict warning to keep quiet. Then he tugged my jeans and briefs down, freed my aching cock, and wrapped his fist around me, stroking me with his right hand while he fingered my hole and whispered nasty sweet nothings in my ear. I came like a geyser, shooting ropes of cum on my chest. When I eased my middle finger from my entrance, I realized this statistics thing might be a problem. How was I going to survive months of lusting after my tutor?

"Just tell him how you feel," Max advised matter-of-factly.

"Are you nuts?" I snorted derisively. "That would be a disaster."

I furrowed my brow at Max in the gym mirror, pleased that my physical reaction to him had dwindled over the past year since we broke up. I couldn't deny Max Maldonado was extraordinarily hot, though. He was six one with short dark hair, olive skin, and green eyes. And his body was a thing of beauty. Everything about him was perfectly proportioned, from his ears and nose to his ass and his gorgeous cock.

Considering our history, it was pretty damn amazing that we'd managed to find our way back to "just friends." We'd known each other since we were toddlers. Our mothers belonged to the same church group. They studied bible verses while their babies fought over primary-colored blocks in the classroom next door. According to my mom, we were fast friends, but that wasn't how I remembered it. Max bugged the hell out of me. He was a class clown with the attention span of a gnat. He never meant any harm, but he always seemed to cause trouble. You know the type. The kid who accidentally pulled the fire alarm, set the classroom pet hamsters free, and poured melted M&Ms into the teacher's purse. I was the opposite...a goody-goody who avoided conflict at all costs. I steered clear of him until sometime around my thirteenth birthday when my traitorous body began to notice him in a completely different way. And crazy enough, he noticed me too.

Max was my first everything. Kiss, hand job, blowjob, anal… you name it, we did it. We danced around attraction and a slow-growing friendship for a few years. Nothing happened between us until we were sixteen. And then, we were inseparable. We were able to explore our shared sexuality by pretending to be best buddies when truthfully we were a couple of horny teenagers who, somewhere along the way, became real friends. And for the short time that our physical intensity and friendship meshed, I thought he was "the one." He wasn't, but that was okay. On days like today, when my mind was spinning over Rory, I was grateful I had someone I could talk to who wouldn't ask a million dumb questions.

"Does he have a nice ass?" Max asked, raising his brows lasciviously.

Never mind. Some things never changed.

"Yes, but that's not the point," I huffed, wiping sweat from my forehead with the back of my hand. I picked up a set of weights and moved to stand beside him.

"Maybe not, but it's a perk. Be honest, Christian. If the guy was a twerp, you'd find excuses not to meet him. Then you'd convince yourself that you could study on your own and turn your grade around. And when it got harder to do than you thought, you still wouldn't ask for help because you're a stubborn dickwad with too much pride. If you ask me, you need a sexy distraction to help you focus."

"That makes no sense." I lowered the weights, pausing to shoot another irritated glance at him.

"Sure, it does. It works for you now. You're surrounded by hot guys in tight football pants every day. The more stress you're under to throw the ball to the right receiver, the better you do. You've always been like that."

"Thriving under pressure isn't the same as looking for trouble."

Max set his weights on the rack, then crossed his arms and gave me a thorough once-over. "Ooh. What kind of trouble are we talking about? Did he say he wanted to fuck you?"

I spun around so fast, I made myself dizzy. "No! And what the hell is wrong with you? Lower your voice," I hissed, setting the weights down.

"Lighten up, Chrissy. We're the only ones here besides the old dude on the leg press. He can't hear us over his public radio podcast," Max admonished. "You're always five steps ahead when you don't have to be. Don't marry the guy in your head. You don't even know if he has a boyfriend."

"I saw him kiss another guy, but he said he's single."

"Guys lie all the time. In this case, it doesn't matter. If you actually get laid while studying a subject you hate, you wind up in the win column. Am I right?" He held his hand up for a high five.

I ignored his hand and rolled my eyes. "Nothing is going to happen."

"If it does, let it. You're free to do whatever and whomever you want. Like me."

"Wait. What's up? Did something happen with you and Sky?"

"I don't know." He pursed his lips and then twisted to face me. "Something doesn't feel right. I don't know what it is, but it's there."

Wow. I'd come a long way. Nine months ago, I would have been torn between being thrilled his relationship was in jeopardy and wondering if there was still a chance for us. Now, I was more concerned about splitting the rent between two people instead of three if Sky moved out. I set aside my financial worries and refocused on my friend.

"Is there someone else?" I asked gently.

"No. It's not like that. It just feels different. Like we're together but not in the same place. You know what I mean?"

No, I didn't. Especially since I'd heard them having rather vocal sex before I left for practice that morning. Squeaky bedsprings, loud groans, and the inevitable "Fuck me harder, Max!"...in other words, the usual.

"I'm not sure."

"Me either. All I know is, I feel like I can't breathe lately. He's always around and, I should love that 'cause I want to be with him but...I guess I need space too."

"Can you tell him that?"

Max snorted. "Yeah, right. He'll think I want to break up. That's not what I want. I just want to be alone sometimes. Or I want to hang out with you without him getting jealous over nothing."

"He's exhausting," I blurted with a sigh.

"True, but he's hot as hell and the sex is—"

"Yeah, yeah. I hear the sex. Often. We don't need to discuss it." I stood and glanced at my watch. I had fifteen minutes before I had to get ready for class. I didn't want to waste it talking about my replacement.

"Can I say this stuff to you, or is this weird?" he asked, furrowing his brow.

"You can talk to me, Max. It's not weird at all," I said sincerely.

Max threw his arm around my shoulder and squeezed me against his side.

"Good. I'm really glad we can be honest with each other 'cause I have something to say to you. Are you listening?"

I wiggled out of his hold and punched his bicep. "No, I'm not."

"You should, 'cause I'm about to give you some great advice."

"What is it?"

"Fuck the tutor."

"Excuse me?" I asked incredulously.

"You heard me. Fuck him. Let him fill your brain with numbers and equations and then ask him to fill your—"

"Do *not* say another word," I growled, taking another peek around the deserted gym.

"I'm stating the obvious, dude. You need sex more than anyone I know. If you have a crush on the guy, why not see if he feels the same? The worst he can say is no."

"Wrong. The worst he can do is tell my coach...you know, the guy who set this up. If Perez heard that I propositioned my tutor for a booty call on the sly, life as I know it would be over," I grumbled unhappily.

Max scratched his chin thoughtfully. "Be subtle. Don't straight up say, 'Dude, let me suck your cock.' Lead up to it. Seduce him. You remember how to do that, don't you? If it's mutual, he won't out you to your coach or anyone else. At least think about it."

I opened my mouth to blast him for giving me lame advice, but really, I should have known. Max had developed a Nike-esque mentality about sex over the past year. If any opportunity arose, pun intended...it was a "just do it" moment. Not my style. I knew he and Sky had a semi-open relationship with a host of rules that gave them each a green light to act on temptation. I tried not to ask too many questions. It was strange enough living with my ex and his boyfriend. I didn't need to know any details. But I sure as fuck wasn't going to adopt his newfound groovy-love mentality and potentially screw up my future. Not when I was this close to the finish line.

"Thanks, Max...but we've officially reached the point where I'm going to do the opposite of whatever you suggest."

"Okay, then my advice is to pay close attention to the textbook bullshit and not stare at his dick in his tight jeans."

"With any luck, he'll wear baggy basketball shorts and it won't be an issue."

Max barked a quick laugh and picked up another set of weights. "You love guys in basketball shorts. You even like it when they wear leggings with them."

"It's hot."

"No, it's not," he countered.

"Yeah, it is."

"No, it's not."

"Oh, my God. Why do I hang out with you?" I griped without heat.

He paused midcurl to meet my gaze in the mirror. " 'Cause you love me, and someone's got to remind you to have fun once in a while."

"I don't love you, and I have plenty of fun on my own."

"Don't ruin my day. You totally love me. But your social life needs work. You suck at having fun. Going to postgame parties and fakin' it with a few cute girls isn't a good time. Treat yourself with the new tutor. Or...come play with me."

"What does that mean?" I asked warily.

"Let's go to LA, hit a few bars where no one knows us, and just...get lost for a while. Come on. We haven't done that in forever. Just me and you."

"What about Sky?"

"I'd rather go alone. Just us."

I held his gaze for a long moment, then nodded slowly. "Sounds like you're asking for trouble. But maybe you're right."

Max grinned at my reflection in the mirror before offering a fist bump. "Good. Then it's a bro date. Just like old times."

"Hmm. I can't go this weekend. I have an away game. And if things get busy with my classes, I—"

Max groaned aloud and flattened his hand over my mouth. "Don't be a buzzkill and don't overthink. It's going to happen.

That's all that matters. Batman and Robin will be back in action."

I snorted. "Who's Batman in this scenario?"

"Me," he quipped with a roguish smile.

"No. I'm not going unless I'm Batman," I countered.

"You can be Aquaman."

"No one wants to be Aquaman, asshole."

Max shook his head. "I'm Batman. You can be Superman or..."

I chuckled as he ran through every superhero he could think of. Max was right. Maintaining sanity was important, and a little outside diversion in the form of "something to look forward to" might be good for me. If it kept me from worrying about passing statistics with the help of my unexpectedly sexy tutor...even better.

2

Hiring Rory wasn't really a question. I couldn't argue with the expense or his credentials. Coach Perez informed me that the athletic department would take care of my new instructor's fees and that he'd personally contact my counselor to assure her I was receiving the extra help I needed. Of course, the proof would be in my grade. I failed my last quiz so spectacularly that my teacher pulled me aside afterward to ask if everything was okay in my personal life. Talk about alarming. I had to ace next week's test and at this point, my only hope was the sexy man staring out the coffee shop window, nursing a cup of ice water.

"Hi, there. I'm sorry. I hope you haven't been waiting long," I said, setting my backpack on the empty chair across from him.

Rory started before glancing up at me with a slow, lopsided grin that made my heart skip a beat. I couldn't help noticing how his royal blue T-shirt matched his eyes and hugged his muscular arms, showcasing the colorful ink on his left bicep. Damn, he was hot.

"Nah, I'm early. There wasn't much traffic today, so I made good time. You ready to get to work?"

"Uh, yeah. I'm gonna order an iced coffee. Do you want anything?" I asked, gesturing toward the counter at the front of the store. Thankfully, on a Tuesday afternoon, it wasn't overly crowded.

"I'm cool with water."

I frowned and shook my head. "My treat. What do you like? Latte, coffee, tea, hot chocolate?"

He held up his hand to protest. "That's okay. I—"

"I insist."

Rory shot a sideways glance at the posse of giggling teenage girls entering through the side door. "Why?"

" 'Cause I don't like drinking alone. Hurry up. If they get to the front before me, this will take forever. I need caffeine. Stat."

"Latte. No foam," he replied with a grin. "Thanks."

I took my place in line behind a pretty young girl with long black hair. She turned to give me a flirtatious once-over that was more predatory than charming. However, I should have thanked her for reminding me I had a role to play. I doubted I'd run into anyone I knew at a Starbucks twenty minutes from campus, but I couldn't let my guard down—regardless of where I was or who was likely to notice me. And I was already doing a bad job. Ignoring a cute girl while casting nervous glances at Rory was all kinds of gay. Wasn't it?

I pulled my cell from my pocket and scrolled through old texts just as a new message from my father popped up. It was short but direct.

I have a meeting with the dean at the law school. Hopefully your application will be all that's required for admittance in the fall. I'll let you know how it goes.

Fuck.

"Next in line," the barista called.

I placed my order, then moved to the side counter to wait for our drinks and respond to the text before I had to deal with a completely different kind of distraction.

Thanks, I typed.

Shoot. Was that enough? I didn't want to seem ungrateful, but I didn't want to seem too eager either. Neutrality was key when dealing with my father. Or anyone, really.

I snuck a peek at Rory and froze. His eyes were locked on me like he was sizing me up and trying to figure me out. There was nothing overly personal or unprofessional in the look—just curiosity. He smiled when he caught my gaze and suddenly, nothing seemed more important than being in the moment.

I stuffed my phone into my pocket, picked up our drinks, and made my way back to the table.

"Here you go," I said, handing the latte to Rory.

"Thanks. Let's get this party started. Did you bring your last test?"

I retrieved it from my backpack, wincing as I slid the paper to him. "It was ugly."

He widened his eyes and let out a low whistle. "Damn. Did you at least get points for writing your name at the top?"

"Ha. Ha." I dropped my bag on the floor and sat down before adding, "I wish. I could use the extra credit."

"Hmm. Let's see your book."

I dug my textbook out and set it on the table, then settled back in my chair to study him while he assessed the enormity of the challenge he'd taken on. His brow creased as he alternately flipped through the pages and glanced at the questions on my last quiz. I shifted in my seat, hoping to clandestinely ease the pressure of my dick against my zipper. Call me crazy, but the promise of being treated to nerd-speak from a badass former wrestler was the stuff of dreams. I sipped my iced coffee as I admired the intricate inked script along his wrist. I leaned forward slightly to get a better glimpse, but it appeared to be written in another language.

"Do you speak Spanish?" I asked.

Rory did a double take, then inclined his head. "A little. Do you?"

"No."

"All righty then," he replied with a half laugh before glancing down at the book again.

"Do you still wrestle? I mean, competitively?"

Rory pushed the book to the middle of the table and grabbed his latte. He fixed me with a roguish stare and took a sip. Then he set the cup aside and leaned forward. "I thought we already did the 'get to know you' thing the other day. Do you really care if I wrestle anymore, or are you stalling 'cause you think I'm gonna berate you for getting a crappy score on your test?"

I puffed up my cheeks like a blowfish and nodded. "Yes."

Rory chuckled. "Okay, let's chat. I'm not here to make you feel bad about what you don't understand. I'm here to help. In normal, everyday shit, I'm not known for my patience, but when I'm teaching, it's different. I'm fucking Gandhi here, you know? I want you to learn. So don't think I'm judging you. I'm not. I'm on your team. I'm not gonna spank you for getting a bad grade."

I licked my bottom lip and before I could stop myself, said, "That's strangely disappointing."

Rory opened his mouth and closed it theatrically. "You're flirtin' with me."

"No! No, of course not. I—"

I shook my head effusively and sucked on my straw until I gave myself an iced-coffee brain freeze. I hoped when the feeling passed, I'd come up with the perfect one-liner to turn my awkward faux pas into a joke. I pushed my cup aside and gulped. Nope. I had nothing.

"You're not what you seem, are you?"

"Sure, I am. I'm a typical dumb jock. I can tell you anything you want to know about football, but don't ask me about Pythagoras's Theorem," I said, elevating my dork status to tragic levels in a single blow.

Rory's eyes crinkled at the corners as he hooted with laughter. "Pythagoras's Theorem? So what you're really saying is that you're a kinky-ass geometry geek who happens to know how to throw a football. Good to know."

I crossed my arms and waited out a new round of merriment. "Are you finished?"

His shit-eating grin lit his eyes and made him look impossibly handsome. *Dammit.* If I couldn't get through fifteen minutes without making a fool of myself, I was screwed. And not in a way I might like.

"Yeah. I'm sorry. No more laughing." He snorted. "Tell me what you know about Pythagoras's Theorem."

"I don't know anything. I remembered the name. That's all," I admitted.

"Hmm. You lie to me, you'll end up across my knee in no time," he teased. At least I thought he was teasing. His broad smile and twinkling gaze invited me to stop taking everything so seriously, but I was too embarrassed to find anything funny.

"Right," I replied primly. "Should we get started?"

"Hold up. We've got to clear the air here. It's like I told you the other day, you won't retain anything until you relax. So let's see...you wanted to know about Spanish and wrestling, am I correct?"

"It's not important."

"Maybe not, but I think it's a good idea to use ten minutes to get more acquainted and—"

"We did that last week," I argued.

"Well, it didn't stick, so let's try it again. What'd you do over the weekend?" Rory asked conversationally.

"You don't want to hear about my game or the stupid college parties I went to, so let's talk statistics." I tapped the cover of the textbook meaningfully.

"We'll get there. Did you win?"

"Yeah, it was a blowout."

"Sorry, the acoustics in here are whack. Did you say you got a blowjob?"

I snickered, then sat back and twisted the straw in my to-go cup. "Unfortunately, no."

Rory tsked. "Too bad, my friend."

"Did you?"

"Yep. I want to brag and tell you it was amazing, but it wasn't all that special. I was horny. He was willing....You know the story."

"Yeah, I think it's called a short story with a happy ending," I joked.

"Ha! Exactly. That's what happens when you go lookin' for love in da club. Everyone's out for a quick fix. Sounds perfect until it's over ten minutes later. Then you gotta deal with the uncomfortable 'Did we really just do that?' aftermath. Not so fun. Enjoy college life while you can. This adult business sucks," he huffed humorlessly. "And yeah, I took Spanish in school and my brother speaks it. I know enough to hold a short conversation. That's about it. Why'd you ask?"

I frowned. "I don't know."

Rory gave me a patient look. "Talk to me, Christian. We covered Basic BS 101. You told me you won your game and went to a coupla boring parties. I told you I went to WeHo with some friends. Now I'm backtracking to your question about whether or not I speak Spanish 'cause I'm polite like that. Plus it was a weird one. Why'd you want to know?"

"Your tattoo," I replied, gesturing at his wrist.

Rory turned his palms over for me to inspect. "They're lines from a Pablo Neruda poem. This one says, '*En mí todo ese fuego se repite*' and this says, '*En mí nada se apaga ni se olvida*.' The translation is, 'In me all this fire is repeated' and 'In me nothing is extinguished or forgotten.' The poem is called 'If You Forget Me,' and it's poignant as fuck. If you don't know it, look it up."

"I will. That's cool." And "poignant as fuck," as he so eloquently put it. "But what does it mean to you?" I asked.

"That goes a little beyond water-cooler talk, QB. We'll save it for when and if we get to know each other well enough to tell secrets," he said, winking to take the sting from his words.

I nodded in understanding but instead of pulling away, I absently reached out to touch the script. Then I looked into his eyes, and I could have sworn I saw the tiniest crack in his armor before an invisible shield fell into place. In that fraction of a second, a silent communication passed between us. He'd been through hard times and he'd emerged...possibly stronger than ever. I was curious for sure, but there was no way to politely ask his story, so I inclined my head and switched gears.

"Did you study poetry in college?"

"No." Rory sat back and eyed me for a long moment before continuing. "Are you ready to tackle stats now?"

I slumped in my chair with a theatrical sigh and gave myself a mental high five when he chuckled at my antics. "Ready as I'll ever be."

"I'll go easy on you. I've got a feeling this is gonna hurt me more than it'll hurt you," he snarked.

I chuckled at the playful innuendo as I leaned forward, intent on giving him one hundred percent of my attention for as long as I could possibly stand it.

Forty minutes later, I had to admit Rory was a good teacher. He'd obviously considered my mental block for all things math. Instead of trying to force concepts and equations down my throat, he came up with relatable everyday scenarios and applied them to his lesson. Although after going through two very involved problems, my brain needed a break.

"I think that's enough stats for the day," he said, closing the textbook. "Your eyes are starting to cross."

"Hmph. True. But I marginally understood what we covered, so that's not too shabby. If you add anything else, I'll just get confused."

Rory scoffed. "The reason you get confused is that you mistakenly think one equation will solve everything. You're looking for shortcuts and there aren't any."

"Why not? There should be CliffsNotes for every facet of life," I said, only half-kidding.

"The more you practice, the easier it gets. But you can't skip any steps. Look at it as though you're a private investigator gathering information to crack a cold case file," Rory suggested. "Each clue gets you closer to solving a murder."

"Bad analogy. Murder mysteries make me nervous."

He cocked his head thoughtfully. "So math, murder, and pretty girls who stare too long make you jumpy. Anything else?"

I glanced around the sparsely populated coffee shop and furrowed my brow. "Who's staring at me?"

"The high-school girls and the woman who was standing in front of you in line. They've all left now. They gave up when they realized you only had eyes for me," he teased.

"Hmph. Yeah, right. I doubt they thought we were a couple," I commented, shaking the leftover ice in my cup.

"Why not? Statistically speaking, there's a chance that's exactly what they thought." Rory waggled his thick brows comically.

"Very clever. But I bet the average gay couple doesn't hang out at a Starbucks poring over a textbook." I narrowed my eyes. "Why are you looking at me funny?"

"I'm trying to figure you out. Would you care if they thought we were boyfriends or a Grindr hookup?"

"Of course not," I lied, stuffing my book into my backpack. "But I don't think we look like boyfriends or a Grindr hookup."

"You're awfully concerned with the way things look, aren't you?"

I sputtered indignantly. "No, I'm not."

"Relax. I'm just giving you a hard time," he said with a laugh. "But I will say this...if we were a Grindr hookup, we'd probably give ourselves away with the 'We just did it' look."

"Did what?"

"It." He made a lewd "finger in hole" gesture and then laughed at my perturbed expression.

"Right," I huffed indignantly and glanced away, hoping to hide the certain blush on my cheeks. My dick twitched at the very idea of doing "it." I had to get us back on track quickly, or I'd be doomed. I patted the textbook in my backpack and said, "Where? In the bathroom?"

He shrugged nonchalantly. "Yeah."

I was more fascinated than flustered now, which made no sense. His cocky delivery alone should have set me off and tripped every one of my personal alarm bells. Joking about gay sex with my new tutor was unwise. Sure, it was my favorite topic, but that info was top secret. If I were smart, I'd change the subject. Fast.

"What makes you think I'd have sex with you in a public restroom?" Nope. Not so smart after all.

" 'Cause that's how hookup apps work. They're basically dating apps in reverse. Only simpler. Sex first, then coffee. Dating sites are hell, if you ask me. First you match up and agree to meet. Then you cross your fingers and hope to fuck his online photo isn't a decade old and that when he said he liked cats, he wasn't a creepy cat guy."

I snorted a laugh. "What's a creepy cat guy?"

"Oh, man." Rory shook his head in mock consternation. "You know the type. He owns ten or more cats and insists on showing you the YouTube videos he's made for each one on his phone. And when he tells you their names, you notice that each one has a special voice. Carol, Mike, Marsha, Greg..."

I threw my head back and guffawed. "Wait a sec. They're named after *The Brady Bunch*?"

"Yeah, well done," he commented with a laugh. "A lot of people our age don't know classic sitcoms."

"My parents were strict about TV viewing, but the Bradys made the cut."

"Hmm. Well, back to the crazy cat guy."

"I thought he was a creepy cat guy," I intercepted.

Rory shot a mock scowl at me but inclined his head. "Yeah, whatever. This guy names his cats on a theme. TV shows, rock bands, favorite songs..."

"Seems kind of harmless. What's wrong with that?"

"Nothing...but it's hard to have a conversation with that guy," Rory explained.

"Why? Cats are cool. And coffee dates aren't a big deal. I don't see the problem."

"You're being difficult on purpose," he huffed. "I didn't say cats aren't cool. I happen to have a very cool cat. But she has a normal cat name, and I don't make weird noises when I say her name."

I leaned on my elbows, aware that my smile had taken over my face. I should have checked the time and thought about getting back to campus for my second practice, but I didn't want to go anywhere. This was surprisingly...fun. I couldn't remember the last time I'd talked to anyone about something other than football or my "future." Okay, Max was easy company too, but this was different somehow. Rory was...unexpectedly charming.

For a tutor. And now that he'd hinted at all these interesting things that had nothing to do with statistics, I wanted to know more. Much more.

"What's your cat's name?"

"Buttons," he replied, looking out the window.

I snickered. "Why Buttons?"

" 'Cause she's cute as a button, and what the fuck are you laughin' at?" he asked in a mock-serious tone.

I wiped tears from the corners of my eyes and shook my head. "You. I can't keep anything straight. You're built like some of the burliest linebackers on my team, but you're smarter than all of them put together. Brawn, brains...and a cat named Buttons. I can honestly say I don't know anyone like you."

"You forgot gay. Let's not forget that's how this conversation started," he singsonged.

"It is?" I asked, sobering immediately.

"Yeah, I told you if we were a hookup, we'd have already had sex. Things went a little sideways after that."

Rory popped the lid off his to-go cup and raised it in a mock toast. I studied his Adam's apple and let my gaze wander from his large hands to his powerful-looking arms. And just like that, my dick had a pulse of its own. I licked my lips, willing myself to pull it together 'cause he was talking now and I couldn't hear a fucking thing.

"What did you say?"

"I said I'm sorry." He cocked his head and gave me a pirate's smile. "I think you know I'm just playing with you, but I have a rep for saying things I shouldn't. So if I offended you, I apologize."

"I'm not that easily offended. And I thought your creepy-cat date story was very entertaining."

"It was hypothetical. I don't date."

"Why not? You didn't seem to like that last blowjob you got

in da club," I teased. "Maybe you should give a little pre-sex conversation a try."

Rory scoffed. "You're hilarious. The BJ wasn't so bad. It was just boring."

"How is a blowjob boring?" I asked incredulously.

"When it's..." Rory circled his hand expressively. "...routine. Like when your partner is just going through the motions. Open mouth, close eyes, moan, fondle balls, twirl tongue around the head, give partner a sexy 'This is about to happen' look and then deep throat cock until he gags."

I swallowed hard and tried to think of a response that wouldn't advertise the fact that I was now sporting major wood. I'd been half-hard since I'd put my textbook away, and the unexpected fellatio play-by-play didn't help.

"Sounds like maybe you're looking for love in the wrong places," I said with a nervous-sounding half laugh.

"Thankfully, I'm not looking for love anywhere. I'm so bad at relationships, it's almost funny," he said.

"Me too. Good thing I don't mind my own company."

Rory squinted and gave me a shrewd once-over before gathering our trash. "Quarterbacks get all the action, Christian. Something tells me that if you're spending time alone, it's 'cause you want to."

"Maybe. I'm too busy either way," I replied vaguely as I picked my backpack up off the floor and hiked it over my shoulder.

"Same."

I followed him to the front of the store and held the door open for him with my elbow as I pulled out my phone to check the time. This was a good place to make my exit. But once again, I found myself asking one more question to keep him talking. "Have you been single for a while?"

"Yeah. My ex dumped me a year and a half ago. Honestly, I

can't blame him. I was such an asshole. I didn't mean to be, but I wasn't ready to be totally out. He's better off now anyway." Rory paused and gave me a funny look. "This is kinda weird, but I bet you know Mitch's boyfriend."

"Huh? Who's Mitch?"

"My ex. He's been with his new guy for a year, I think. Evan... I forget his last name. Something Italian. He graduated from Chilton last spring and he was a football player, so you must know him. It was a big deal when he came out. It was all over social media."

I stopped in the middle of the sidewalk and gulped as I turned to face him. No fucking way could the world possibly be that small.

"Evan di Angelo? You know Evan?" I asked in a small voice.

"Yeah. He works out at the Y. We've actually become friends. He didn't like my status as the ex at first, but we're cool now and —hey, you okay? You look a little pale."

I swallowed around the desert in my mouth and nodded. "I'm fine. And yeah, I know Evan. We're friends. He's a good guy."

My tight-lipped smile wasn't convincing, but Rory had no reason not to believe me. He scratched his head as he backed up.

"Right. When's your next quiz? We've got to get you an A."

"Um, Friday. I think," I said distractedly.

"You think?" he prodded.

"I'm pretty sure. I'll let you know."

"Text me. We can come here again or figure something else out." He fished his keys from his pocket and squinted at me. "You sure you're okay?"

"Positive. I'll touch base with you tomorrow. And thanks. This was helpful." This time I thought my smile was sincere.

Rory nodded, then set his sunglasses on his nose and headed toward an ancient black pickup truck. I watched him for a few seconds. Or more accurately, I stared at his ass. And because timing was everything, he turned before he opened his door and gave me a knowing smile. I gave him a harried one in return and raced to my car.

I revved the engine and glanced in my rearview mirror as he pulled his truck into the exit lane. He rolled his window down and rested his arm on the ledge, tapping his fingers along to whatever he was listening to on the radio. I licked my lips and took a deep breath.

I didn't get it. I was around guys like Rory all the damn time. Athletes with big muscles and healthy egos to match. Something set him apart. He wasn't like anyone else I knew. And he was on to me. I could tell. He hadn't blurted "You're gay," but he'd let the conversation drift to places he knew would make the average straight guy cringe. Maybe he wanted to make me uncomfortable, but somehow I doubted it.

And he knew Evan? Fuck me. Statistics was turning out to be my worst nightmare in more ways than one.

MY SCHEDULE WAS PRETTY REGIMENTED; I did well with guidelines and rules. I'd been that way since I was a kid. My parents were strict and while they certainly had a lot to do with my sense of personal discipline, the rest was me. I liked being in control. And let's face it, on a football field, the quarterback controlled everything in the offense. He called the plays and drove the action. If a QB did his job well, a run resulted in points and just like with any other game, the more points you scored, the more likely you were to win.

I liked being part of a team. I always had. Working with a group of friends toward a common goal was a powerful feeling. When I stepped onto the field with my teammates, I was instantly part of something bigger than myself. I didn't get off on being in charge, but I was good at it, if I did say so myself. Even though I was the one calling the shots, I knew nothing happened if we weren't all on the same page.

My dad claimed I was a lot like him. Not in an athletic sense. He was a self-proclaimed geek who got off on tidy spreadsheets and balanced budgets. He had a take-charge attitude when it came to finance. Oh yeah...and butting into my life.

Maybe that wasn't entirely fair, but at the moment, it felt like it. I secured my towel around my waist as I glanced at the incoming message on my phone and grimaced.

Call your father, Christian. Love, Mom

I wanted to be amused by my relatively young mother's formal style of texting, but her message bugged the hell out of me. This was how my parents communicated. My father made a broad declaration, and Mom made sure my sister and I got the message. No doubt to avoid aggravation later. Don't get me wrong—my dad wasn't a bad guy. He was compulsive about details, order, and attention. I knew his heart was in the right place. He wanted me to succeed, which I totally appreciated. But I resented his heavy-handed style of inserting himself into every facet of my life. I was an adult, for fuck's sake.

It was one thing for him to be somewhat aware of my class and practice schedule, but he didn't need to know every minor detail in between. Or maybe I was aggravated that they'd disturbed my Rory-infused daydreams.

I'd thought about him nonstop since Monday afternoon. I was nervous about meeting him again and at the same time, I couldn't fucking wait. I studied nonstop and occasionally texted to ask him questions when I got lost on a problem. Maybe he was on to me. Maybe he knew I'd never cracked a math book this many times within a forty-eight-hour period in my life and that the only reason I did so now was to have an excuse to talk to him.

Wow. I was a head case.

I typed a quick message to my mom, letting her know I'd call Dad on my way home; then I shoved my cell into my bag. I used a little more force than necessary, which caused an avalanche of events. First, my phone fell on the locker room floor. Then I stepped back to pick it up and bumped into someone behind me. And then...I accidentally stripped his towel off when I tried to steady myself.

Let's be real. Nudity in the locker room was a nonevent. We'd seen it all and then some. Conversations about ball placement and tackling techniques while washing your junk in the shower didn't faze anyone on the team. But there was always one idiot who couldn't pass up an opportunity to make a stupid joke.

"Jesus, Christian," Jonesie scowled, readjusting his towel.

"Sorry, man," I said absently.

"If you wanted another peek at the goods, you coulda just said so."

I rolled my eyes. "I didn't."

"Well, if you change your mind, I'll be right over here." He batted his eyelashes and gestured toward his locker, which unfortunately was located directly across the aisle from mine.

I gave him a sharp look as I swiped some deodorant on. "Good to know, but...no thanks."

"Hey, never say never, man," he singsonged.

Here's the thing about guys like Jonesie. He was a stereotypical jock who gave the rest of us a bad name. He was loud, boisterous, and overbearing. He tended to think his role as a starting lineman entitled him to a variety of perks, like star treatment at school events and private parties—including free alcohol and the adoration of all the "hot babes." His words, not mine. He wasn't a bad guy; he was just a little dumb.

What he lacked in brains, he made up for in brawn. He was two inches taller than me and at least eighty pounds heavier. And most of it was muscle. His love of football and his considerable ego were assets on the field, but in everyday life, he could be irritating as hell. As team captain, I'd become a master at the art of deflecting stupid and keeping order in the locker room. I knew that sometimes the best method of dealing with a bonehead like Jonesie was to ignore him.

So I wasn't quite sure what I was thinking when I responded with, "Sorry. You're not my type."

Jonesie gasped in mock dismay. "I'm crushed. It's cool, though. You don't do anything for me either. Your tits are too small." He paused to slap high fives with Moreno, a fellow lineman and if possible, a bigger bonehead than him. "You know, since Evan graduated we lost our token gay dude. One of us has to go 'mo, fast. We gotta have a rainbow mascot. It's good for business. We were all over the news last season."

"That was 'cause we won the championship," Moreno reminded him.

"Yeah, but the homo factor got us a spot on the five o'clock news." He pushed his hand through his short brown hair and looked around the locker room. "Who's it gonna be? Jackson, Andrade, Kawinski...?"

"Shut the fuck up, Jonesie," I growled impatiently and for emphasis, I chucked my deodorant at his chest. I might look scrawny next to the guy, but I had a rocket for an arm.

"Fuck, that hurt!" He grimaced as he hopped backward, covering his right pec. "You know I'm kidding, man."

"Well, don't. Evan wasn't a token gay anything to this team. He was a beast of an athlete who helped lead us to that championship."

Jonesie held up his arms in surrender. "Geez, okay. It was a joke. I love Evan, dude. I got nothing but love for *all* the gays since he came out. I mean, he didn't look or act queer at all. He was just one of us."

I nodded curtly, then yanked my towel off and stepped into a pair of black boxer briefs. Then I reached for my jeans, hoping he'd clue in that the conversation was over.

No such luck.

"You know, I can't even picture him with another guy but whatever...at least we know he's the man in his relationship. I can't see Evan letting anyone stick their dick in his ass," he continued conversationally.

Nervous laughter twittered around us. I think everyone knew I was pissed that he hadn't dropped the discussion, but they were hopeful I'd find a middle ground and ideally not lose my cool. I zipped my jeans, then wiggled my fingers, silently requesting him to pick up my deodorant and hand it over. He obeyed without thinking and let out a squeak when I twisted his wrist and fixed him with a menacing stare.

"Are we done here?" I growled in a low voice.

Jonesie held my gaze and nodded. "Yeah."

Someone turned a Kendrick Lamar song on just then and belted out the lyrics at top volume. Within a minute, everyone was either singing along or talking over the din. And though it might not feel sincere, the atmosphere at least gave the illusion we'd returned to "normal."

I finished dressing, hiked my strap over my shoulder, and stopped to give Jonesie a friendly pop on his arm. The guy was like an overgrown puppy. He hated being called out, but he disliked being out of sorts with anyone even more. Particularly me. If I walked away without a word, he'd beat himself up and be miserable the rest of the day. Ultimately, that wouldn't be good for any of us. When he grunted in acknowledgment, I made my way to the exit, pulling my cell from my pocket.

My run-in with Jonesie had fired me up. This was probably

the perfect time to chat with my occasionally caustic father. I hesitated for a beat before throwing my bag onto the back seat of my Prius. Then I scrolled for his number and pushed Call.

"Hello, son. I see you got my message."

"Hi. Um, yeah. I just got out of practice."

I braced myself for the inevitable question about where I'd been beforehand and why I hadn't returned his call sooner. But he had other things on his mind—specifically, how to take over my future.

"That's nice," he said dismissively before continuing in an excitable tone. "I spoke to the dean of the law school today."

Great.

"O-kay."

It wasn't okay, but he wasn't interested in how I felt. And he didn't require much input from me, so I put the car in drive and headed home, grunting occasionally to let him know I was listening.

Ten minutes later, I parked in the lot next to my building and made my way to my place. The grounds of our complex had a Spanish-style-meets-contemporary design that Max and I both liked when we first decided to live together. Tall palm trees dotted the landscape and red bougainvillea added splashes of color along the stucco façade. I took the stairs to our third-floor apartment, so I wouldn't accidentally cut off my dad's call in the elevator.

"...if you complete your application by early November, I can personally hand-deliver it to the admin at the law school. She'll want to see your transcript too."

"Dad, you're supposed to take the LSAT first. I won't have time to do that until after my season ends," I reminded him, sliding my key into the lock.

"I know it's a lot, but if you started studying now, you could take the exam in late November. The timing would be ideal. By the beginning of the year, you'd have your near-term future set. You wouldn't have to move or make any big changes. Of course, if you wanted to save money and live at home, you're welcome to but—"

"Okay, thanks for the info. I'll look into it," I lied, pushing the door open.

I was immediately greeted by a low groan and desperate-sounding erotic dialogue.

"Please, baby, more. You feel so good."

"Oh, God! Oh, fuck. Oh, yes—"

Holy crap! I scrambled to step outside and shut the door on the live-action porno happening in my living room. Hopefully before my father noticed.

"Where are you? It sounds like someone is hurt," Dad commented.

"Uh, my neighbor is blasting his television again," I replied, wincing at the muffled groans still audible through the front door.

"Hmph. Your apartment seems noisier than it used to be. You and Max should consider moving or—"

"It's fine. Don't worry. Um, I should go. I have a lot of studying to do."

"Good. That's the spirit! I copied you on the email to the dean. Take a look at it and we can talk later."

He disconnected the call before I could reply. I cast my gaze from my cell to my doorknob, wondering how much time I should give them to finish up. Dammit, I hated when Max and Sky pulled this shit. I counted to ten, then inched forward and listened at the door for a few seconds before slowly opening it.

Apparently I was in time for the post-sex cuddle fest. Max's arms and legs were wrapped around Sky and his hips moved in a languid rolling motion that probably meant he'd had an out-of-body orgasmic experience and wasn't in a hurry to come back to reality. I hated that my dick instantly wanted in on the action. But who could blame me? Max and Sky were a gorgeous couple.

They were tall, handsome, and both were built like gods. Baseball gods specifically. They'd met last year when Sky transferred to Chilton. He was the much-anticipated new shortstop our school's team needed, and Max couldn't stop talking about him. Sky was fast, funny, and he loved sci-fi movies. Max hadn't mentioned Sky was also extraordinarily hot. He was blond, blue-eyed, and had golden skin that complemented Max's dark good looks. I knew I was considered handsome, but I had nothing on those two. And the day Max brought his new "friend" over, I knew our time was up.

It had hurt like hell for a while, but not now. In fact, I was strangely immune to my current situation. I stood in the foyer watching my ex-boyfriend fuck my replacement on the IKEA sofa we'd bought together with a sense of hard-won detachment. I wasn't jealous anymore. I could admit they looked hot together. And I just hoped they'd remembered to put a towel on the cushion before they got busy.

"Hello," I called out with an absent wave. "Don't mind me. I'm just going to get something to eat and download some porn in my room."

I set my bag on one of the barstools and skirted the small island before making a beeline for the fridge. I grumbled under my breath about inconsiderate roomies, controlling parents, and jackass teammates while I foraged for food. The container of leftover chow mein looked like my best bet. I grabbed a fork, two bananas, and a water bottle, then turned and immediately bumped into Max.

"Hey, sorry about that," he said with a mischievous grin.

I grunted, giving him a thorough once-over. His bare chest glistened with sweat, and his black shorts hung low on his hips, showing off his prominent V-line. I glanced into the adjoining room at his boyfriend, who was sprawled naked on the sofa, scrolling through messages on his cell with his spent cock on full display. Sky's hair was artfully mussed, and he had a rough-looking bite mark on his shoulder.

"Fuck you, Max," I grunted without heat. "You're not sorry. Why fucking pretend?"

He furrowed his brow and cocked his head in confusion. "Are you really pissed or mildly irritated?"

"I don't know what I am, but you're hopeless. I've never met anyone who thinks with his dick quite like you." I sighed heavily and shook my head. Then I lowered my voice and continued. "Didn't you just tell me you thought this was over?"

"Shh!" he admonished, casting a quick look toward his boyfriend before refocusing on me. "I don't know what we're doing. I told him we should take a break after practice today."

"That's your idea of breaking up?" I set the food on the counter and then opened the container of chow mein and took a healthy bite.

"Well, I tried," he whispered. "He didn't like it, but he agreed. Next thing I know, we're naked. Dude, we've done it three times in two and a half hours. Shower, bed, sofa. Maybe he's trying to kill me with sex."

I made a grossed-out face and rolled my eyes. "You're un-fucking-real."

"Nah. I'm just horny." Max shrugged, then reached over and pulled a noodle from my container. He flinched when I poked his hand with the fork. "Ow!"

"Back off, Max. I'm going to study."

He grabbed my elbow before I got anywhere. "Don't be mad, Chrissy."

"I'm not mad. I just had a crap day," I huffed but softened my tone before adding, "Look, maybe I should get my own place."

"No!" Max winced, then took a deep breath just as Sky called his name from the living room. "Look, we got carried away. It won't happen again. Don't talk about us not being together. It's too...sad."

"Max, we're friends, but he's your boyfriend and this feels weird. Like he wanted me to walk in on you guys. Think about it. You told him you wanted to take a break, and I bet you told him that you and I were going to LA without him." I gave him a chance to deny it before letting out a heavy sigh. "He's jealous, Max. And I don't want any part of your drama. You don't get to have your cake and eat it too."

"What if it's chocolate?" he joked, capturing my chin and then pinching my cheek playfully. "Maybe you're right. I'm sorry. I'll talk to him."

I swatted his hand away and opened my mouth to blast him, but my barbed reply wouldn't come. Max couldn't help being Max. And truthfully, some part of me admired his single-minded quest for pleasure and his ability to live in the moment.

"Fine. Keep it down. I'm going to study."

I bumped my fist against his, then gathered my belongings and called out a short greeting to Sky.

"Hi, Chrissy. Hey, don't worry. We put a towel down. I insisted."

"Gee, thanks, Sky. How about putting your tightie whities back on too?" I singsonged as I made my way to my bedroom.

I put the bananas, water bottle, and chow mein on my desk under the window. Then I turned on the lamp, drew the blinds, and hurried back to close my door to muffle the sound of their conversation.

This was crazy, I mused as I unearthed my statistics textbook from my backpack. I was trapped in my room with cold Chinese food, a math book, and probably a dozen emails from my dad reminding me to think seriously about my future in the profession he'd chosen for me. I flipped through my stats homework with glazed eyes and absently reached for my phone, intending to listen to some music to drown out my roommates and the errant thoughts in my head.

But at the last second, I pushed Rory's number instead.

"Yo."

The monosyllabic grunted greeting made my mouth go dry. *Fuck.* What was wrong with me? I licked my lips nervously, hoping I could talk without squeaking.

"Hey, Rory. It's Christian."

"Christian," he repeated in a raspy tone that sounded like sex personified. "I know. Your name popped up on my caller ID. What's up?"

"Um. I'm...I have a new assignment," I blurted. "It's supposed to be a simple, four-part question but it's confusing."

"How so?"

"Well, there're a lot of numbers."

Rory's melodic laughter floated across the line, warming me from the inside out. I felt my shoulders relax and was instantly glad I'd called.

"Numbers aren't your thing, eh?"

"No, not at all. I don't trust problems that disguise themselves as simple stories but turn into complicated messes. The gist of this one is, two friends go to the market with *x* amount of money and specific items they must purchase for a recipe. There's a formula for earning more cash and ways to buy alternate brands. And supposedly, somewhere in there is an actual question."

"Makes you wish for the days you could count your fingers to come up with the answers, I bet. Read it to me. Let's see if I can help you break it down on the phone."

"Are you sure? I don't want to bug you."

"You're not. I'm standing in front of the sushi section at

Whole Foods, wondering if I should choose the spicy tuna or eel. What d'ya think?"

"Spicy tuna," I replied automatically. I flopped onto my desk chair, kicked my shoes off, and then swiveled to prop my feet on my bed.

"All right. Done. So what's your problem? Tell me all about it."

I chuckled at his tone. I just wanted to hear him talk. He sounded like a sexy therapist...if that was possible. The deep timbre of his voice soothed me and kept me grounded in a way I couldn't explain.

"My math problem or my real-life problems? Never mind. Real life takes too much time."

"I'm heading for the ice cream section now. I've got time."

"Hmm. Well, one of my teammates pissed me off, my dad is continuing his quest to take over my life and...I just walked in on my roommates having sex on the sofa. Shall we move on to the math problems now?"

"Max and Sky? They're a couple? They're gay?"

"Yeah. And they're all over the map. One day, they're in love and the next, it's tension city. But they usually make it to their bedroom before they go at it." I almost added that I suspected Sky timed their fuck session with my arrival home, but it sounded paranoid and would likely invite more questions than I wanted to answer.

"Rude. That's what I like about living alone. Buttons would never pull that shit on me," he huffed. "What should I get? Chocolate Chunk or Cookies and Cream?"

I snickered merrily. "Chocolate Chunk, of course."

"Of course. Now, what problem are you stuck on? Read it to me and..."

I opened the book and recited the equation with a ridiculous smile on my face. And just like that, I felt like myself again.

Rory and I met a half dozen times over the next couple of weeks at the same Starbucks. I wouldn't claim that my comprehension of statistics got better with each session, but I felt like I was making a mental breakthrough of some kind. I didn't panic when a lengthy word problem asked for the dreaded median, mean, and mode. I simply took a deep breath, plotted out the best course of action, and got to work. My efforts didn't always result in a correct answer, but my quiz scores improved from total crap to moderately stinky. I certainly wasn't out of the woods, but I was beginning to think there was a decent chance I might pass statistics and graduate as planned.

I might not like the subject, but I liked Rory. A lot. I looked forward to our coffee-shop meetings. He always arrived before me and somehow commandeered the same table overlooking the parking lot. We traded off buying each other's drinks. It wasn't something we talked about. It just evolved, like a funny tradition you looked forward to without realizing it had become a "thing." I'd either hand over his latte, no foam, or he'd slide my iced coffee across the table as I flopped into my chair. We'd tap our to-go cups and make small talk about the weather, the traffic, my most recent game, his kids at the Y, or his job search. Once he declared it was time to get to work, there was no goofing around.

Rory's mission was to help me pass, and he was determined to make it happen. He had a way of assessing my moods and encouraging me to keep going when he could tell I was ready to give up. He exuded a Zen-like aura of patience and serene calm that didn't quite match his tatted bad-boy exterior. But the second he closed the textbook, he morphed back into the slightly intimidating hunk with rough, prickly edges and a bawdy sense of humor. He fascinated me. And yes, he turned me on. But I couldn't be sure if it was the naughty twinkle in his eye or his obvious intelligence that got to me. Whatever the reason, I was more than inspired to keep my end of the deal and show up on time, ready, and willing to learn.

Until my eyes crossed and I couldn't concentrate anymore.

"...divide x into y to find the variable and—hey, did I lose you?" Rory asked, snapping his fingers in front of my nose.

"Letters turning into numbers. My brain can't take it," I groused woefully as I slumped in my chair.

Rory closed the textbook, then leaned forward and patted my hand. It wasn't much contact, but I felt like I'd been zapped by a rogue electric current. I met his gaze and swallowed hard when my heart beat like a drum. I was all for having an excuse to touch him or stare at him, but sometimes his nearness overwhelmed me. Or maybe it was just his hotness. I did my best to tune in when I saw his lips move.

"...done for today. Let me know how you do."

"How I do what?"

Rory snorted. "Wow. I really did lose you. Text me after your quiz. If you can remember anything that stumps you, we'll try to go over it again before your big test next week."

I sighed heavily. "I doubt I'll remember anything. Geez, I'll be lucky to make it out of there alive. I have a game tomorrow. I can study over the weekend."

He regarded me for a long moment before speaking. "Is your game local?"

"Yeah."

"Hmm. Maybe I'll come."

"To my game?" I sat up tall and furrowed my brow, instantly alert and confused as hell.

Rory chuckled at my wide-eyed expression. "Yeah. You know, I've seen you play."

"Really? When?"

"A few weeks ago. Sometime after we'd first started this tutoring gig," he replied casually.

"You should have told me you were there."

"Dude, the stadium was a madhouse. It's already small, and they pack 'em in like sardines. I couldn't have announced myself without climbing over a dozen people to get to you," he huffed.

"Oh. I wish I'd known." I kept my voice low. I wasn't sure he actually heard me, which would have been fine. I sounded wistful, and that was all kinds of embarrassing. "Why didn't you tell me sooner?"

"I don't know. I mean, it was a homework assignment for me in a way. I wanted to see you in action and get a feel for your style of play. You were on fire that night," he said with a smile. I was immensely pleased with his admission until he added, "Evan told me you were cool under pressure. Easily one of the best quarterbacks he knows."

"You talked about me with Evan?"

"Yeah. We weren't exactly gossiping, but he knows I'm tutoring you." Rory frowned. "Is that a problem?"

Fuck, yes. I wiped my suddenly damp palms on my jeans and shook my head. "No. Not at all."

"Well, anyway, I decided it was time to see for myself. I

bought a ticket at the gate and ended up sitting next to your fan club. A bunch of girls screaming your name at the top of their lungs. It was brutal. By some freak miracle, I managed to tune them out and concentrate on the game. You specifically."

"Me specifically?"

"Yes, you're the guy who controls the action on a football team with a winning record. Our mutual friend claims you've got ice water in your veins when a posse of giant defenders comes at you, but I get the guy who flinches at the sight of a math problem."

"Ha. There are a lot of people like me."

"Maybe, but you're the only one that matters to me."

I knew he didn't mean it the way it sounded, but that sentiment, paired with his piercing gaze, did something to me.

I shifted on my seat and pursed my lips thoughtfully. "What did you find out?"

"You're a fucking great quarterback who sucks at math," he deadpanned.

I threw my head back and laughed. "I'm pretty sure I told you that a few weeks ago."

"No, you downplayed what you excel at and made it seem like you're desperate to graduate and get the hell out. Which is kinda interesting. Most people at the top of their game are all about dragging out their glory moment. Not you. Why?"

"I'm a realist. This game is fun and I love it, but I know my limits. My arm is good, and my aim is generally on target. But you have to be exceptional to make it to the pros and unfortunately, a great third-division quarterback doesn't always make it to the big league."

"What do you want to do after you graduate?"

"Move. Get a job. Find a place to just..."

"Just what?" Rory prodded.

"Be free," I said softly.

Rory nodded slowly and observed me for a moment. "I know what you mean. But from what I could tell, you seem free on the field. You're in a zone when you're out there calling the shots. You're relaxed. Shoulders down, eye on the prize, ready for battle. Leader of the offense. You don't notice the crowd, the opposition, the lights, the fans. You're completely focused. It seems natural."

"It *is* natural. I love football. I hate this stuff." I thumped my hand on the textbook and glowered.

"That's okay. Not everyone likes it. And not everyone is a leader. We all have different strengths. The point is, you seem like the kind of guy who has no limits. You can do anything you want and be anything you choose to be. You're lucky. Once you figure out how to channel that energy, you're going to be unstoppable."

I stared at him in surprise. I hadn't expected that sort of speech on my behalf. Sure, I'd had coaches and teachers tell me I showed promise. But it felt different coming from Rory. It felt as though he saw a part of me that I'd forgotten. Something intrinsic that had nothing to do with my sport or my sexuality.

"Thank you."

"Don't thank me. Just be true to yourself." He held my gaze, then snapped his fingers and winked. "Oh yeah...and relax. You're too fuckin' uptight."

I burst into laughter. "I am not."

"Yeah, you are. I get the impression that after football, you spend a lot of time overthinking shit you can't do anything about. When was the last time you did something for yourself that was just for fun?"

"Um, I don't know. I might head to LA after my game with Max. He wants to go to a few bars or clubs."

"What kind of clubs?"

"I don't know. He likes places where the deejays are the main draw." I named a few, chuckling when Rory rolled his eyes.

"My brother bartends at one of the new 'places to be seen.' I hate that shit, but my drinks are free, so it's hard to resist. If you end up on the west side, check out Vibes and ask for Justin. He'll take care of you."

"Hard to refuse free alcohol. But we might not go to LA at all. There are a few parties here and—"

"You should go," he insisted.

"Why?"

"It's like I told you earlier. You need to relax. And I bet you a million bucks it'll help your math game."

"I really don't see how that's possible." I chuckled.

"Trust me, grasshopper. I'm smart about this stuff." Rory tapped his forefinger against his temple. "If you can stand the crappy music, it's all good."

"It's dance music," I scoffed. "What's wrong with it?"

Rory made a face. "Everything is electronic. It sounds the same after a while."

"What kind of music do you like?"

"Classic rock. What about you?" he asked.

"I like everything, but I probably listen to classic rock the most. The Cars, Bon Jovi, Bruce Springsteen."

"Me too. I love even older stuff, like The Beatles and Stones too. And I have a soft spot for eighties music too. I love The Cure."

"Same. What's your favorite Cure song?"

"Boys Don't Cry," he replied quickly. "They're more our parents' era. My mom loved their music until she found religion and decided to cut out lead singers who wore makeup from her playlist."

"Her loss."

Rory smiled. "I think so too. What's your favorite Cure song?"

"Just Like Heaven."

"Everyone says that one," he teased. "Give me another one. What was your...?"

I leaned forward with my elbows on the table and a sappy grin on my face. I could have done this all day and all night long. Just sitting across from Rory, talking about silly things I rarely shared anymore felt significant somehow. Like a new beginning. Like we were both in the same place, wanting to know so much more about each other than our usual ten-minute chat before tutoring allowed.

As thirty minutes bled into an hour and then two, we blocked out the excess noise from our table next to the window and lost ourselves in whimsical conversations that had no rhyme or reason. The most insignificant details seemed so damn interesting. I wanted to know his favorite color, movie, cereal, and TV show. And when he said, "Green, *The Godfather*, Wheat Chex, and *The Office*," I wanted to know why. We analyzed our preferences and debated their merits good-naturedly before moving on to the next topic. I couldn't get enough. And something in his eyes told me he felt the same way.

Rory's self-deprecating candor made me laugh. I'd never met anyone so unapologetically in tune with himself. My cheeks hurt from smiling. I probably looked like a lovesick puppy. No doubt he knew I had a crazy crush on him. I wished I were brave enough to come clean and tell him who I was and how I felt. I wasn't ready for words, but I found myself leaning in more than necessary to be closer to him. When our knees touched under the table and our fingers brushed as we moved our empty cups, we went still and silent.

And that was when I knew words might not matter. He knew

I was gay, or maybe bi. He knew I liked him. But he wasn't asking for anything in return. For now, this was enough.

———

THE GAME SATURDAY afternoon wasn't well attended. The normally crowded stadium was only half-full. There were a few different factors to blame. Our opponents were the lowest ranked team in the league, the weather was unseasonably cool for mid-October, and bigger names were playing at the same time. I was pretty sure UCLA and USC were both in town. But this was the only game that mattered to me.

I called a huddle in the middle of the fourth quarter, glancing toward Perez on the sideline before addressing my teammates.

"We're gonna run number four. Moreno, box out my blind-side. Don't let anyone through," I instructed gruffly.

"I got it, boss. They're a bunch of fuckin' pansies. My grandma could handle these idiots," he scoffed.

I shot him an annoyed look, then motioned for everyone to get in position. When the ref blew the whistle, I called the play again and clapped briskly to signal we were ready to begin. I caught the football; then I stepped back into the pocket and scanned the field, looking everywhere at once. My plan was to wait for Gonzalez to run twenty yards before launching it to him. The backup was to hand it off, but I figured we go with that play next and run some time off the clock. The score was twenty-eight to zero. With six minutes left in the game, I wasn't concerned with adding more points. I just wanted to stay on the field for as long as possible and hopefully win in a shutout. But the second I cocked my right arm back, I sensed trouble. I secured the ball and glanced sideways just as a ginormous defender breached the line and made a mad dash for me. I made a narrow escape and slid out of reach only to get pulled down from behind. I fell hard on my right knee and the lineman who outweighed me by at least fifty pounds toppled like a tree on top of me.

Okay, here's the thing...football is all about forward momentum. Not every play worked every time, and we all knew it. But this one should have worked. The only reason it didn't was because a few of my guys were already celebrating this win. So yeah, even though the score didn't change, I was pissed. And though I knew our head coach would yell at Moreno and whoever else messed up, it was my job to back him up. A quarterback led on *and* off the field. I was in charge of revving up the team before games and congratulating them for a job well done. If there were issues, I was expected to point them out. And the second we were back in the locker room, I did.

I called a quick powwow, congratulating the guys on our win. Then I showered, changed, and iced my knee before confronting Moreno on his faux pas.

"I'm sorry, man. I thought Jonesie had you."

I removed the ice bandage wrapped around my knee and left it on the bench before glaring at Moreno. He looked like a sullen child who got caught with his hand in the cookie jar. But there was an angry edge to his attitude too. I couldn't tell if he was mad at me or himself, but it didn't matter.

"Don't blame anyone else. That was on you. If you can't handle your position, have your grandma call me. Maybe she can do it better than you," I scolded, hefting my bag over my shoulder.

My mind whirled as I headed for the parking lot. I picked apart the plays we'd run and thought about how we could have executed them better. I had a slate of Xs and Os in my mind with imaginary red arrows pointing in varying directions. I nodded and waved to a few familiar faces as I dug my keys out, but I didn't slow down until I reached my car and noticed the large man leaning against the truck parked next to me in the nearly deserted lot.

I stopped in my tracks as Rory straightened to greet me. Warmth seeped through my body, and a huge smile I couldn't seem to contain spread across my face.

"How's the knee?" he asked.

"Fine. What are you doing here?"

"I told you I'd be here, remember?"

"Yeah, but...I'm surprised you stayed. It wasn't a great game," I said, opening the trunk and tossing my bag inside before sidling between our vehicles and leaning on my Prius.

There wasn't much wiggle room. I could practically feel his body heat in the confined space. And damn, it felt nice. I crossed my arms and tried to maintain some semblance of cool. It felt strange to see him here...but good.

"At least the stands weren't crowded. No screaming fans chanting your name in my row. It was mayhem in the next section, though. You're a rock star here," he commented with a laugh.

"Ha. I d-don't know ab-bout that, but—"

"You're freezing." He reached out to rub my arms, then dropped his hands quickly and opened the passenger-side door of his truck. "Get in. Just for a second. I won't keep you. I promise."

I hesitated for half a second, then obeyed, closing the door just as he opened the driver's side and climbed in. "Much better," I sighed. "You aren't here to quiz me on that test, are you? I haven't studied at all."

He turned on the engine and blasted the heat before shifting to look at me. "Nah. Believe it or not, I just wanted to say hi."

"Hi." I smiled shyly, marveling at my wild mood swing. I

couldn't remember what I'd been thinking about before I bumped into him.

The lamplight cast a shadow over his profile in the twilight. I could still make out his features, but he looked mysterious somehow. And sexy. Very sexy.

"So what happened out there? One minute you were dancing around the field looking for a target—and the next you were on your knees." He waggled his eyebrows lasciviously.

I knew he was joking. Inappropriate humor was Rory's way of dealing with awkward situations, but I wasn't in the right frame of mind. Sitting next to him in his truck felt oddly intimate. I could almost imagine we were at a cozy table for two at a romantic restaurant. I wanted to stare into his eyes and ask about his day. I wanted to find excuses to touch him while I told him about mine.

I fixated on the hand he'd draped lazily over the steering wheel as I collected my thoughts. Then I launched into a brief summary of what had happened during the play.

"This is what you get when you celebrate a win before the final whistle is blown," I griped. "I told Moreno to focus, but... whatever. I'll be fine. I just need some rest and maybe something to eat."

Rory nodded, then glanced out the rear window. I followed his gaze, noting the empty parking lot. "Do you feel like getting a burger or something?"

"Are you asking me out?" I countered with a half smile.

I expected him to roll his eyes and make a snarky comment about the concept of "dating." But he didn't. He went perfectly still and then inclined his head slightly. "Yeah. I think so. Or would that be weird?"

"No. It would be nice."

"Nice," he repeated, furrowing his brow. "The thing is, I didn't really mean it in a *nice* way."

"You want to ask me out in a bad way?" I teased.

"Definitely, but the tutor thing might feel strange. Does it?"

"I don't think so," I replied carefully.

He held my gaze for a long moment, then pursed his lips. "Okay. Well, where do they have good burgers around here?"

"Rory."

"Yeah?"

I swallowed hard and gave the same cursory look out the window he had before leaning across the console. Then I grabbed the collar of his denim jacket and crashed my mouth over his. It wasn't so much a kiss as a frenetic fusion. My heart raced and my skin felt too tight and yet, somehow this felt right. And it only got better when he held my head and pulled back slightly to soften the connection. He bit my bottom lip before deftly pushing his way inside, gliding his tongue alongside mine in a slow, sensuous motion. I groaned aloud and angled my chin to get closer still.

Oxygen was overrated. This was all I needed. The slow tangle of tongues, his fingers in my hair, and the soulful sound of an old Aretha Franklin song in the background. I had no idea how long we made out in the front seat of Rory's truck. I only knew I could have happily done it all night long. It was crazy, because as much as I wanted this, it didn't seem possible. In fact, there was a small part of me that was afraid this might be a dream. I wasn't going to be the one to end it.

Rory finally broke for air and rested his forehead on mine. He sat back and regarded me cautiously as if mentally preparing himself for me to freak out.

"I didn't mean to do that," he said in a gravelly tone.

"Actually, I kissed you first," I reminded him.

He flashed me a wicked grin that made his teeth look impossibly white in the moonlight. "You did, didn't you?"

We shared a poignant smile I desperately wanted to quantify.

I was terrible at measuring gestures of affection though, so it was probably a good thing my cell buzzed just then.

I pulled it from my pocket and glanced at the message. "Shit. I forgot about Max. He's waiting for me at home."

I rattled off an unnecessary explanation about my impatient roommate wanting to get on the road to LA as I clandestinely adjusted my erection.

Rory nodded. "You should go."

"Yeah." I opened the passenger door and stepped outside. I started to say good-bye, but at the last second, I paused. "What are you doing tonight? I mean, if you're free, maybe you could go to LA too and..."

"Meet you at the bar?" Rory finished with a wicked grin.

"Yeah."

"I'll see you there."

"Good." I held his gaze before closing the door and waving good-bye.

He waited like a perfect gentleman for me to get in my car and pull out ahead of him before following me out of the parking lot. I snuck a sideways peek at his truck as he turned onto the main street. Then I set my fingers on my swollen lips in wonder.

Something was happening here. I hadn't felt this way about a guy in years. Lightheaded, vaguely nauseous, and slightly dopey. I wanted to stare into his eyes and hang on his every word the way I had with Max when we were teenagers. But this was different. Rory and I weren't kids. We were grown men. And I wanted things now that I didn't know were possible back then. It was intoxicating to know he felt the same.

———

FOR A KID who grew up in a conservative area in Orange County,

LA always felt like another planet. It was an hour away by car but light years away in every other respect. And West Hollywood was a whole other universe. It was gay wonderland. Every restaurant, bistro, boutique, bar, and club seemed to sparkle with gay glitter dust. Sometimes literally. Same-sex couples held hands and kissed in public. And drag queens and go-go boys drew as much attention as A-list celebrities.

Typical LA artifice ruled. Everyone was freaking gorgeous and seemingly well-versed in fashion trends and who was in and who was not. The judgy factor intimidated the hell out of me. I hadn't braved this neighborhood in years. I wasn't a celebrity quarterback by any means, but Chilton had a decent LGBTQ population for a small school. There was always a chance someone might notice me.

I glanced up at the Vibes neon sign from my place in the long line and bit my lip nervously. I hadn't thought to ask if this was a gay club. *Fuck.* I felt so uncomfortable in the electric blue mesh top Max borrowed for me from his boyfriend's closet.

He'd shaken his head in dismay when I emerged from my room earlier wearing a striped button-down shirt. "You can't go like that. You look like a preppy dork from the OC."

"I *am* a preppy dork from the OC." I held the wispy piece of fabric up and frowned. "Is this Sky's?"

"Yeah, but he won't mind," Max assured me.

"Bullshit. He'll gouge my eyes out."

Max snorted, then inclined his head in agreement. "Okay, well maybe, but he's out of town visiting his family anyway."

"Did your invitation get lost?"

"Permanently lost. They don't like me. Can you believe it?" Max yanked my jacket out of my hands and tossed it over his shoulder. "You don't need that. What are you gonna do, tie it around your waist on the dance floor?"

"It's cold outside," I protested.

"You won't have time to get cold. You'll be dancing."

An hour and a half later, I was freezing my ass off while Max flirted with a pretty-boy dressed in pink in the line outside the club.

"He's hot," he whispered as we shuffled forward.

I nodded absently while I scanned messages on my cell. I wondered if Rory was inside. Free drinks or not, I honestly couldn't picture him here at all. I thought about texting him and suggesting that we meet somewhere else, but then, maybe this was a test of some kind. Yeah, I kissed him, but I hadn't actually come out to him in real words.

"Whatever you're thinking, stop. It was your idea to come here, and I personally think it's one of your better ones," Max said, flashing a sultry smile at the cutie behind me.

"I don't know. It might be a mistake. You have a boyfriend and—"

"And he's out having fun too. I'm sure he'll send me a video later of some random dude sucking him off."

"Ugh. You two are so weird," I groused, canvasing the sidewalk for familiar-looking faces.

"Maybe, but...you've gotta relax, man. No one we know is here. No one recognizes you. You aren't that important. Just enjoy, Chrissy," Max advised, pulling me toward the entrance.

"I fucking hate it when you call me that."

"You fucking love it."

AN HOUR LATER, I loved everything and everyone. I was mildly tipsy, but by no means drunk. I figured one of us should stay somewhat sober, so I sipped my second margarita while I scanned the bar area for Rory and tried to figure out which bartender was his brother. The three men manning the bar didn't look anything like him. One was a sexy pretty-boy who might have been a model, the other was tall and skinny and covered in tats, and the third was Latino with longish brown hair and an edgy urban-cowboy look. Maybe his brother wasn't working tonight, but I wouldn't know until I asked. Or until Rory got here. If he was coming.

It was fine either way. The longer I was here, the more I liked it. The electric energy in the club had a life-affirming, liberating vibe. I felt my shoulders relax as I swayed to the music while watching sexy men writhe and kiss or just talk with their hands on each other's hips. I didn't feel like an outsider. I belonged here, I mused, setting my glass on the bar.

I flinched when someone wrapped his strong arms around my chest from behind. I bit Max's forearm and chuckled when he yelped. He scowled, then leaned across me to place his order.

"Want a refill?" he asked.

"No, thanks. Where's your new friend?"

"Over there." He inclined his head in the general direction of the dance floor and grinned. "Where's *your* friend?"

"I don't know. Maybe he changed his mind."

"He'll be here."

"What makes you so sure?"

" 'Cause I bet he's got as big a crush on you as you have on him. Don't bother denying it. We wouldn't be here at all if you didn't have it bad for your tutor. I can't wait to be formally introduced." Max waggled his eyebrows lasciviously before reaching for the kamikaze he'd ordered from the skinny bartender.

"Max..."

He let out a half laugh and rolled his eyes. "I'll be good. If he doesn't show up, let's find someone else for you. How about that guy?"

I discreetly turned to see who he was referring to and shrugged. "He's cute."

"Hmm. And he's staring at you."

"So?"

"What does 'so' mean? Go introduce yourself." He motioned for me to get moving.

"No, thanks. I'm a bad flirt."

"That's true. Oh, my God, I'll never forget the time you asked that hottie at the frat party what kind of toothpaste he used 'cause his teeth were so white. Classic!" Max threw his head back and laughed at the not-so-distant memory.

"Yeah, well, I didn't want to get my ass kicked if he wasn't like us and...whatever. That *was* embarrassing." I swiped his drink from his hand and took a swig.

"He thought it was funny."

"So did his girlfriend."

Max snorted. "True, and—oh! That's gotta be him. You said muscles, tats, and totally hunky, right? He's talking to the bartender, fist bump, checkin' out the scenery and...he's looking this way. Dude, you undersold the tutor. He's fucking hot."

I twisted sideways, aware of my suddenly erratic heartbeat as I searched the crowd. I gulped nervously when I spotted him pushing through the crowded bar to reach us. *Please don't say anything stupid. Please don't pass out.*

"Funny running into you here," Rory drawled.

His eyes glinted with ready humor, crinkling at the corners. Max was right. He looked sexy as hell. He wore a snug army-green T-shirt that hugged his muscular arms and chest, and his jeans fit to perfection. But his appeal went well beyond looks. Rory had a commanding presence; he took up space when he walked into a room. And at a crowded gay club in the heart of La-la land, he probably looked like someone everyone thought they should know.

"Yeah, what are the odds?" I let out a nervous half laugh and quickly introduced him to Max.

I shot a meaningful look that roughly translated to a plea not to say anything embarrassing. Max smirked but gamely exchanged pleasantries over the din of a Lady Gaga mix. When Rory turned back to me, I could have sworn a private cocoon lowered over us, making it seem like we were alone. He was the only one I could see, hear, or smell.

Rory bumped my shoulder playfully. "What are you two drinking? I'll have Justin get you something."

I held up the kamikaze in my hand and shook the ice. "This is Max's but—"

Max hooked his thumb toward the dance floor. "You keep it. I'll see you out there. Nice to meet you, Rory." He waved good-bye and stepped away before returning to whisper in my ear. "Have fun. Go home with him. I bet he uses a good toothpaste."

He kissed my cheek, then disappeared into the throng of gyrating bodies before I could reply. I sipped the kamikaze as I turned to face Rory.

"It feels weird to see you here," I said lamely.

"I told you I'd come. I'm later than I thought I'd be. Justin needed help moving equipment in my truck. I hope there's a security guard on duty behind the club. He's got an expensive amp, a drum set, and five guitars out there. I'm supposed to help him unload after his shift but...I told him I was meeting you first. I have an hour before I have to go. He's not closing tonight."

"Which one is Justin?"

"The one with the hippie hair," Rory replied. "I'll introduce you later. He looks pretty busy right now."

I glanced toward the crowded bar and nodded. "Is he in a band?"

"Yeah, sort of. 'In between bands' is probably a better way to put it. He broke up with his girlfriend, the lead singer of Gypsy Coma, and then fucked their drummer, who happens to be a guy. She got pissed, threw his stuff out of the studio, and now I'm the U-Haul man."

"Huh. What are the odds of two brothers being bi?"

"Probably higher than you'd think," he quipped before giving me a thorough once-over. "You look hot."

"Thanks. So do you. It seems weird to see you in LA. You belong at that table by the window at Starbucks."

Rory chuckled low and deep. My fingers itched to trace the creases at the corner of his eyes. "Starbucks?"

"Yeah. Did you ever run into one of your teachers at the market or the movie theater when you were a kid and think something felt out of place? I was at Albertson's with my mom once, and we ran into Mrs. Joachim in the produce section. So weird. I thought she lived in my third-grade classroom. I had to pretend she was on a field trip to make the pieces fit. It was traumatic."

Rory's eyes sparked with a ready humor that set me at ease. "I bet. I don't want to ruin anything for you, but the only time I ever go to Starbucks is to meet you."

"Oh." I took another drink and willed myself not to act like a dweeb. I wanted to stare at his muscles, trace his tattoos. And fuck, I wanted his hands on me.

"You must have been traumatized when we saw each other in the parking lot a few hours ago," he joked. "No coffee, no stats book...just me."

"I liked it," I said lamely.

"Me too. How's your knee?"

"Fine."

"Good. Come dance with me."

Rory plucked my glass from my hands before I could argue. He set it on the bar, then slipped his hand in mine and led me through the mass of sweaty, dancing men. Music vibrated, beating in time with my racing pulse. He found a postage-stamp-sized space on the floor and stopped abruptly. We collided, chest to chest, and stared into each other's eyes for a long moment, and then he began to move.

I tried to lose myself in the rhythm, but I couldn't concentrate on anything with him so close. My senses were on fire. I wanted to feel him, smell him, touch him, and fuck...I wanted to taste him again. I swayed awkwardly and smiled. Rory returned the gesture and then leaned into to speak just as someone bumped him from behind. He careened against me, setting his hand on my hip to avoid falling over. I took my opportunity and pounced.

I wrapped my hand around his neck and sealed my mouth over his for the second time that day. And damn, he felt even better than before. Strong and safe but warm and inviting. Rory's hands roamed under my mesh top, up my spine, and then down again to rest on my ass. He pulled me against him as he deepened the kiss and took over. He bit my bottom lip, then licked it before driving his tongue inside. We stood under the haze of strobe lights in the sea of sweaty bodies wrapped around each other, oblivious to anyone else.

Public displays were very out of character for me. On the few occasions I'd hooked up with someone other than Max, we were in dark, secluded spaces. No names exchanged, no emotional currency invested. But I was willing to take a chance with Rory because everything about being in his arms felt right. The slow glide of his tongue, the heat of his body, and his hands on my ass. I wanted so much more. And the boost from the tequila I'd had earlier made me feel brave enough to take it. I yanked his T-shirt up and splayed my left hand on his lower back, then dipped my fingers into his jeans. I didn't get far with his belt in the way, but I did it over and over until he nuzzled my neck and licked the shell of my ear.

"What are you doing?"

"I want to feel your skin. Should I stop?"

"Fuck, no. Come with me," Rory commanded, lacing our fingers and leading me off the dance floor.

We serpentined hand in hand through the crowd, passing the restrooms and a series of closed doors, down a darkened hallway. Rory tried the second to last door and shot a wicked grin over his shoulder when it opened. He flipped the switch on the wall, then quickly closed the door behind me and locked it. I squinted in the bright light and tried to get my bearings.

"Is this a broom closet?" I asked, noting the mops, buckets, and shelves of cleaning supplies lining two sides of the tiny space.

"Yeah. And as long as no one has any major spills out there, we're fine. And we're alone." He nipped my bottom lip and backed me against the door.

I groaned into the rough kiss as I reached for his belt. "Good. I want to see you."

Rory caught my hand on his buckle and shook his head. "Whoa. Not so fast. I have a couple of questions for you first."

"What? Like a test?" I bit my swollen lip and gave him the 'What the fuck' look he deserved. " 'Cause if you ask me anything about averages or medians, I might pass out."

"I'll keep it simple," he said with a gravelly laugh that moved through me like wildfire. "I'm more curious about how straight you are."

He stepped between my legs and traced my jawline with a featherlight touch. I gulped. "Not very."

"Are you bi? A little curious? Or just drunk?"

"No. I'm not drunk at all. I'm...I'm gay." I sucked in a deep breath, then added, "I thought you knew."

"I had an idea," he admitted.

"But no one knows. Only Max and Sky."

"And now me."

"Yes, but I'm not out and—"

"Shh." Rory set his forefinger over my lips and then kissed me softly. "You're safe with me."

I believed him. The very notion that there was another person on the planet who knew who I was made me feel infinitely less alone. Gratitude and lust were an odd but powerful combination. And I had just enough alcohol in my system to encourage me to take what I wanted and deal with the consequences later.

I hooked my fingers around his belt loops and pulled him against me, groaning when his rock-hard cock met mine. Even through two layers of denim, that tease of friction was hot as fuck. I wrapped my arms around his neck and crashed my mouth over his. Then like a total ho, I hiked my right leg around his upper thigh and bucked my hips, loving the erotic slide of his erection against mine. We writhed and humped and licked and sucked at each other until oxygen deprivation became a real issue.

Rory pulled back slightly and set his thumb on my bottom lip. "Fuck, I want to do things to you."

I twirled my tongue around the digit and stroked his length through his tight jeans. "You can do whatever you want. But let me suck you first. Please."

His eyes glazed over like he was in a sensual fog. He nodded profusely, then leaned in to nip my chin as he unbuckled his belt and unbuttoned and unzipped his jeans. The second he lowered the fabric, I fell to my knees and freed his rigid pole from his boxer briefs. Talk about beautiful. He was thick and long, and I couldn't wait to taste him. I glanced up when Rory grabbed a fistful of my hair.

"Go on, baby. Suck me."

Fuck, yes. I didn't have to be told twice. I wrapped my fingers around him, stuck my tongue out, and gingerly licked the tip as I fondled his balls. It was just a tease and maybe a chance to get acquainted with his dick before I got to work. I knew I couldn't do it for long. I wanted him too much. I stroked him with a firm grip, licking him from base to tip and back again with a slight twist of my wrist. Rory voiced his approval in a lusty groan that became a fierce growl when I finally swallowed him whole.

I loved sucking cock. And I was good at it. I just didn't get the opportunity to show off my skills much. It had been far too long since I'd been with anyone. I was sex-starved and it probably showed in my overeager technique. I sucked his balls, one at a time, then flattened my tongue over them before licking his shaft like a lollipop. Then I sucked him all over again, bobbing my head while he urged me on with nasty dirty talk that would have made me blush if I wasn't so busy.

At some point, I undid my own jeans, pushed them down, and pulled my throbbing dick out. I had to. The pressure against my zipper was flat-out painful. I hummed in relief as jacked myself and sucked my lover. Rory pushed at my forehead until I released him; then he pulled me to my feet and drove his tongue between my lips as he reached for our cocks. The feel of his calloused hand and his silken skin against mine was almost enough to push me over the edge. He broke the kiss abruptly and licked his middle finger before cupping my right ass cheek. Then he recaptured my mouth and stroked us in unison while he traced my crack. Of course I knew where he was going with this, but I wasn't really prepared, because when he finally tapped his slick finger against my hole, I fell apart.

I threw my head back and cried out as cum spurted between us, hitting our bare stomachs and running over our fingers. Wave after wave of pleasure rolled through me. I was still in a blissed-out state when Rory released me. He rested his forehead against mine and jacked himself furiously.

"Fuck, I'm gonna come," he whispered in a raspy tone.

He roared, bucking his hips when his orgasm took hold a few seconds later.

I massaged his neck while he trembled, clutching my hips and nuzzling my jaw in the aftermath. The contrasting gestures seemed almost sweet after what we'd just done. I was too spent to analyze, so I gave in and just enjoyed the connection.

Rory pulled back first. He grinned mischievously as he licked our cum from his fingers. Then he reached for my wrist and did the same thing. He traced each digit, pausing to suck my middle finger one last time before cupping my chin and thrusting his tongue in my mouth. The element of sheer carnal nastiness might have been the hottest thing ever. It made me feel reckless. If it was physically possible for either of us, I would have begged him to fuck me against the door. I wanted him inside me, surrounding me and taking me over.

Just as the beginnings of a weird romance danced in my head, Rory stepped backward. He shuffled toward the nearest shelf and tore a couple of pieces from a roll of paper towels. He handed one to me and used the other to clean up before redressing. I averted my gaze as I did the same.

With every passing second, I could feel the tendrils of panic weave through me, reminding me who we were to each other. Student, tutor. Guys who met at Starbucks to talk about statistics. He wasn't a stranger. I knew Rory. I liked him and respected him. I just didn't know how to get back to "normal." Was there a nice way to say "Thanks, see ya next week" to the guy who'd fed me our combined jizz via his incredibly talented tongue? Somehow I doubted it.

I zipped my jeans and buckled my belt, mentally preparing my awkward exit speech.

"So, um...I think it's my turn to buy on Tuesday. How do you feel about pumpkin spice lattes?"

Rory did a comedic double take, then busted up laughing. "I hate that shit. Thanks for asking, though."

"Oh. Well—"

He opened his mouth to respond when someone rattled the doorknob. We heard a muffled, "Why is this locked?" and stared at each other with wide eyes. I put my hand over my mouth to keep from laughing out loud when an aggravated employee smacked the door and grumbled about finding the fucking key.

"We gotta get out of here," he whispered conspiratorially. "That was Justin. He'll know what we were up to in seconds flat. C'mon."

A wall of sound washed over us the second he opened the door. It got louder and louder as we moved toward the bar area. Rory made a series of hand gestures to ask if I wanted another drink.

"No, thanks."

"Are you sure? I'm gonna have to go soon and unload all the crap in my truck, but—"

"It's cool. I'm ready to leave too," I assured him.

He studied me for a long moment. I was tempted to ask what he saw. I didn't feel like myself tonight, wearing someone else's shirt and doing things I rarely did.

"Come meet my brother first, then I'll walk you out." Rory pulled me with him as he sidled up to the bar. He greeted the skinny bartender with a head bob and motioned for him to call the Latino hunk with long hair. "Hey, Jus."

Wow. Looks definitely ran in the family. Although I wouldn't have guessed they were related. Ever. Justin was leaner than Rory, with shaggy dark-brown hair, olive skin, and hazel eyes. They were roughly the same height and both were liberally tatted, but that was where the similarities ended. I offered my hand as Rory went through a quick round of introductions.

Justin shook my hand politely, then gave a harried nod toward a patron standing behind me. "What can I get you?"

"Nothing, thanks," I replied.

"All righty. I gotta get back to work before they start climbing over the bar to serve themselves and—"

"This is the quarterback," Rory intercepted.

Justin stopped abruptly and then cast his gaze between us. "Really?"

"He usually wears clothes that don't have holes all over 'em but yeah..."

I scowled at Rory and was about to explain that the shirt was borrowed, but Justin didn't seem to care either way. He grinned wickedly and leaned across the bar. "He has a big-time crush on you. Hasn't stopped talking about you for weeks. If you need a character reference, call me. My little bro's a good guy. Too damn smart, that's for sure, but I can't hold that against him. Yo..." He turned to Rory. "Do you need my keys?"

"No, I got it. See ya at your place."

"Thanks, man. I appreciate it. Oh, hang on." Justin snapped his fingers and gave me a conspiratorial look. "Someone oughtta tell you he farts in his sleep. Otherwise, great catch. Oh, wait... he leaves his socks on the..."

He was still talking as Rory pulled at my elbow and navigated us to the exit.

"That was a bad idea," Rory griped. "All lies, I swear."

I snickered and pulled my cell out when we stepped onto the sidewalk. I typed a quick message to let Max know I was leaving. Then I stuffed it back into my pocket, and rubbed my bare arms. The fresh air was refreshing, but I wouldn't think so for long without a jacket.

"My sister's like that too. It's all funny until you turn the tables on them," I said with a laugh.

"Is she older or younger than you?"

"Cara is older. How about Justin?"

"Two years older. Since you're probably wondering... different dads, same mom. And no, I don't fart in my sleep," he scowled.

"How would you know, if you're asleep?" I deadpanned.

"Ha. Ha."

I tapped his bicep playfully, then pulled my cell out when it buzzed again. "Max is staying."

"And you're going," he said.

"Yeah, I just ordered a ride and—was today weird? Are we going to be okay when we meet on Tuesday?" I blurted anxiously.

"As long as you don't buy me pumpkin spice...it's gonna be fine. Don't worry."

I smiled and gave him an impulsive hug. "Thanks."

Rory kissed my cheek and inched back as a car pulled up to the curb. "There's your ride."

He linked his hand in mine and moved to the vehicle. I stared at our joined hands, slightly mystified by the boyfriend treatment, but I liked it too much to pull away.

In fact, I liked everything about him a little too much. His looks, his confidence, his sense of humor. But most of all, I liked the way he made me feel. I wasn't sure I could define it yet. It was as though he could see things I never showed when I wasn't on a football field. I gave everything I had in each game, but in everyday life, I avoided confrontation and tiptoed around hard truths. I wouldn't have walked into that club if I hadn't thought Rory would come. And I sure as fuck wouldn't have worn this top.

Maybe the club and the shirt didn't seem like a big deal, but for a guy who'd been buried in a closet for years, it was huge. Just having him near me, offering subtle encouragement, made me feel powerful. And alive.

"I'll see you at Starbucks," I said.

"It's a date."

We shared a smile that felt like a beginning. Then I lifted his hand to my lips and kissed his fingers before turning to the waiting car.

IT TOOK FOREVER to get to sleep that night. I couldn't stop thinking about my day, from the parking lot make-out session to the club. If Rory hadn't had to help his brother, I would have gone home with him or invited him over for sure. No doubt about it. Maybe it was ho-ish, but I didn't care. I'd already jacked off to the memory of sucking his cock and the way he'd pulled me against him afterward. His fingers in my hair and the feel of his body through the mesh. *Fuck.* I fell asleep with my hand on my dick, wearing a shirt that didn't belong to me, just to relive the moment. And while handling my cock was a regular occurrence, I never wore anything except boxer briefs to bed.

I finally started to drift off when I heard a light tap on my bedroom door. Max inched the door open, spilling light from the hallway into my room a second later. I sat up on my elbows and glared at him blearily.

"What are you doing?" I hissed.

"Checking on you. I didn't know if you went home with your tutor or not, and I wanted to make sure you were okay," he whispered.

"I'm fine. Why are you whispering?"

"It's dark. You're supposed to whisper in the dark." Max moved into my room and sat on the corner of my mattress before lying beside me. "Since you're awake, you might as well tell me all about Rory."

"Shh. G'night, Max."

He nudged my shoulder. "Did you know you still have Sky's shirt on?"

My eyes flew open. *Oops.* "Do I? I don't care. I'm too tired."

"Hmm. Me too." Max didn't budge, though. He was quiet for a moment; then he said, "The guy I danced with tonight was cute, didn't you think? He had a weird-ass name. Phoenix. His parents named their kids after the places they were conceived. I think my name would be Tustin. How 'bout you?"

I gave him a blank stare, then slowly closed my eyes. "You like him. Did you get his number?"

"Yeah. I can't do anything about it, though. Unless Sky is in on it."

"I don't get it. Didn't you say he was going to send you a dick pic earlier? Why can't you do what you want too?"

"I can. Sort of. I just promised not to this weekend."

"You guys are weird," I grumbled for the millionth time.

"Maybe."

I opened my eyes. "Max, why are you still with him?"

He laid his head on the pillow, but he didn't answer right away. "I don't know. Let's talk about something else. The guy who drove me home played guitar in some band from the eighties. He sang a couple of their hits on the drive back. He actually had a decent voice. We..."

I groaned and rolled over while Max droned on about music that was a decade old when we were born. He did this occasionally when he was in some sort of turmoil. Talking until he couldn't stand the sound of his own voice was Max's way of dealing with uncomfortable thoughts. I figured he'd go back to his own bed when he was ready.

SOMETIME LATER, I awoke to the sensation of being watched. I thought it might be part of a dream. I didn't feel any sense of danger; it was more of a creep factor. Or maybe it was Max. I turned to my side and frowned. He'd crawled under the blankets at some point and burrowed close to me. I inched away from him. I was mildly annoyed, but he could stay if he didn't hog the covers.

I was about to close my eyes again when something clicked. I stared at the shadow in my doorway and then leaned on my elbow.

"Sky?"

He didn't say anything, but he didn't have to. I recognized his silhouette. He lingered for a half second longer, then closed the door. I rolled my eyes and fluffed my pillow. Those two were ridiculous. I kicked Max.

"Your boyfriend is home. Get outta here," I grumbled.

"Mmmhmm."

I rolled over and pulled the covers over my head when he swatted my hand away. Whatever. Not my problem. I didn't want any part of their drama. I had better things to think about.

4

_____

Every quarterback had his favorite receiver. There might be two or three who played their position well and could be relied on consistently, but there was usually one who stood out. Carson Gonzalez was my go-to guy. We'd been a dynamic duo on the field for the past three years at Chilton. He could read my body language and eye and hand signals and get a feel for which play I'd call before I said it aloud. It was an interesting phenomenon since he barely spoke to me on the field. Then again, maybe that was what I liked about him. I appreciated the art of silent communication after listening to Max and Sky alternately fighting and fucking all day Sunday.

I went to the library and the gym to give them privacy, figuring it was a good way to keep occupied so I wouldn't drive myself crazy thinking about Rory and our closet BJ. I could almost believe I'd imagined the whole thing. Even if it turned out to be fake news, the idea alone had provided serious fantasy material. And my roommates' nonstop sexathon didn't help. I came home to a chorus of "Fuck me, fuck me! Pound me, baby! Harder!" from behind their bedroom door and immediately jumped into the shower and jerked off to visions of Rory above me and behind me. It was almost too much.

For the first time in ages, I didn't mind the weekly Sunday night dinner at my parents' house. My dad's constant harping about my grades, the law school application, and the importance of timeliness got old after the first hour, but he reminded me of what I didn't want, which I supposed was helpful in a way he hadn't intended. With all the excess static in my head, it was a wonder I could still throw a football.

Nah...it actually made perfect sense. The game was my ultimate stress relief. One hundred yards of green marked neatly at ten-yard intervals with a goal post on either end was my personal happy space. When I felt overwhelmed by expectations to achieve more, be more, it was nice to have one thing I could count on. *I honestly don't know what I'm going to do without it*, I thought as I glanced sideways at Gonzalez.

He ran down the field and made a sharp left at the forty-yard line before continuing along the side. I pulled my right arm back and unleashed the football. It spun in a beautiful spiral, arcing high at the midpoint before falling gracefully into Gonzalez's arms. He didn't break stride to look for the ball, and he didn't stop running until he reached the end zone.

In a game, it would have been a perfect touchdown. The crowd would have gone nuts, and the bench would have whooped gleefully while an excited announcer sang my praises. "Rafferty does it again! A sixty-yard pass right in the bread basket! That boy is NFL-bound for sure!" Reality was a tad more subdued. My backup QB gave me a fist bump and chuckled when Gonzalez spiked the ball and did his usual TD dance. But everyone else was too busy running through their own drills to notice. And they were probably ready to go home anyway. We'd been in the weight room and then on the field for two hours.

Coach Flannigan blew the whistle and signaled the end of practice just as Gonzalez jogged back to me.

"Oh, I thought we'd try that one more time," he said, sounding disappointed.

"Why mess with perfection?" I joked.

He frowned as he passed the ball over. "It wasn't quite perfect. I had to speed up at the end to catch it. We gotta get the drop to match velocity, ya know?"

I scoffed. "Engineering majors suck."

Gonzalez chuckled. He was a good-looking guy with dark, unruly curls and a lean, compact body. He was smart, athletic, and enthusiastic. And his quiet confidence was laced with a wisdom that seemed like an anomaly among most twenty-one-year-olds.

"My art history minor balances out the geek stuff," he replied with a self-deprecating shrug.

"No. Sorry. Still geeky," I teased as I headed toward the sideline.

"Wait up! I have a question. Um...do you know Sky Jameson?"

"He's my roommate. Why?"

"I thought so. You must have eaten his leftovers 'cause I overheard him talking about finding out his roommate was gay after class. I know Max lives with you too, but I don't think he meant him. It was more like he wanted me to hear so I'd confront you. I don't think anyone paid attention to him. Well, maybe Moreno. He's pissed you yelled at him the other day. He'll get over it and —it's not a big deal, but I thought you'd want to know."

"Uh...right, thanks," I said distractedly.

Gonzalez patted my back companionably, then switched topics to Monday Night Football. We dissected the teams playing that night as we headed to the locker room. I had to give myself credit for a masterful acting job 'cause I didn't give a fuck about the Redskins' chances with their new QB. All I wanted was to run ahead so I could call Max and find out what the hell was going on. But I had more work to do first.

I gave a rah-rah speech about last weekend's game and added something about the tougher competition coming up. I tried to keep it positive while pointing out that we needed to make improvements. I sensed the residual sullenness from Moreno that Gonzalez warned me about, but he was a big boy. He'd get over it before the next game. Or he wouldn't play.

Once my team captain duties were complete, I showered, dressed, and raced to my car to call Max.

"What's going on with Sky and you? Carson Gonzalez said Sky outed me in his art class and—"

"Huh? What are you talking about?"

"You heard me, Max." I tossed my bag onto the back seat before getting behind the wheel. "He made it sound like he specifically wanted the guy on my team to wonder if I'm queer. This must mean you broke up again, and that little shit is on a mission to get some kind of warped revenge."

"Well, he was pissed when he caught us in bed, but we worked it out and—"

"He didn't 'catch us in bed!' That sounds so creepy. We were fully dressed, for fuck's sake!"

"Yeah, but you were wearing his shirt and he got pissed. I guess I had that other guy's cologne on my skin. Sky thought it was yours and...it escalated from there."

I groaned aloud. "Look, you need to sort your shit out with him and leave me out of it."

"I'll talk to him again," Max said in a defeated tone before adding in a rush, "I just—he came out to his family this weekend. It didn't go well."

"Oh."

"I know. And I think he was hoping I'd say I was ready too."

"What did you say? Do you want to come out?" I choked.

"No way! Maybe that makes me a dick, but my baseball career will be over before it begins if I come out. I'm not ready for that." He sighed heavily, then continued. "Don't worry, Chrissy. I'll talk to him. I'm heading home now and I bet you are too, but could you just give us an hour alone?"

"Yeah, but I'm moving out as soon as I find a place. I can't deal with seven more months of this bullshit, Max. He's too volatile. I have enough on my plate right now."

"You're not going anywhere. Just let me talk to him and work this out."

"Fine. Text me later."

I disconnected the call, then swiped my damp palms on my jeans and pulled out of my parking space. I wasn't sure what to do now. I was hungry. I could grab something to eat and get started on my stats homework. It would give me an excuse to call Rory. I needed to hear a friendly voice who'd joke with me about seasonal latte flavors. Someone uncomplicated and unexpectedly kind. And someone who, after two days apart, hopefully didn't think Saturday night was a big mistake.

I stopped at the next red light to check my Bluetooth setting, then I scrolled for his number, and pushed Call.

"Yo."

I gave a half laugh. "Do you always answer your phone like that?"

"Yeah, I'm a man of few words. I s'pose you are too. You've been ignoring my messages."

"You only left me one. I think it said, 'You okay?' And yeah...I'm okay."

"Good. So, how many messages was I supposed to leave?" he countered.

"Three."

"Why three?"

"It's the perfect number. One is too casual, two could be a butt dial, but three indicates active interest without seeming overboard."

"That's a very detailed estimation. And three just happens to be the number on your jersey. I know you're not into numerology. You must be superstitious."

I chuckled. "I am. Comes with the territory. Are wrestlers superstitious?"

"Some are. Not me."

"I didn't think so. You're too practical to be superstitious."

"True. I walk under ladders on the regular and I own a black cat. Actually, she owns me. I'm kind of her bitch. Whatever she says goes."

I burst out laughing and suddenly, I was very glad I'd called Rory. "Buttons is black?"

"Mostly. She has a white paw. She's pretty damn cute."

"I bet."

We were silent for a moment until Rory spoke again. "Are you sure you're okay?"

"Yes."

"Good. Whatcha doin' now?"

I slowed behind a red Corvette and prepared to turn into a neighborhood strip mall on University Street. "I'm going to grab something to eat and—"

"What are you hungry for?" he intercepted.

"Uh, I don't know."

"Do you like pasta?"

"Sure. Why?"

"Come over."

"Now?"

"Yeah. I'm making fettuccine with chicken and veggies. The water is boiling for the pasta and the chicken is still in the oven.

If you come now, it'll still be warm when you arrive. Do you have your statistics book?"

"Yeah, but—"

"Perfect. You're hungry, I've got food and a cute cat you oughtta meet. Your call, though. No pressure."

I nodded mutely and smiled, though the gesture was lost on him. "That sounds awesome. Thank you."

"Cool. I'm easy to find," he said before rattling off directions. "Call me if you get lost. See you soon, QB."

RORY LIVED in a decrepit-looking square stucco building that dated to sometime around the middle of the last century. Rusted ironwork trimmed the doorways of the otherwise plain façade. It might have seemed ornate and charming a few decades ago, but now it looked like dingy lace pasted on cement. I glanced at the clumsy banister leading to the second story before carefully making my way up the stairs. A single fixture between plain doors cast a dull light in the open corridor. I noted the cobwebs along the ceiling and on the dead cactus plant next to his neighbor's door. Pieces of an argument filtered above the hum of traffic from the nearby freeway. And if I craned my neck I could probably see the Nike billboard I'd passed when I'd exited. This place reminded me of a sad motel or a set for a spooky Halloween movie. I knocked at apartment 2B and almost jumped out of my skin when the door swung open immediately.

"Hey, there."

"Christ, you scared me," I said, clutching the strap of my backpack with a scowl before meeting Rory's amused gaze.

Damn, he was sexy. His eyes crinkled at the corners, softening his chiseled features, giving him a boyishly handsome look that went well with his snug retro Bugs Bunny T-shirt and workout shorts. I bit the inside of my cheek to keep any involuntary murmurs of approval to myself.

"Sorry about that." Rory chuckled and widened his arms in welcome. "Come on in. Dinner's ready."

I stepped inside and inhaled the delicious aroma emanating from the galley kitchen to my right. "It smells amazing."

"I'm a fuckin' awesome cook." He winked playfully before heading to the stove to light the burner under a pan of vegetables.

"And so modest too. Can I do anything to help?" I asked, setting my backpack on one of the two barstools at the narrow counter space.

"Nope. As soon as the veggies are sautéed, we'll be ready to eat. Want something to drink?"

"Yes, please. Water is fine. Where's Buttons?"

Rory pulled a water bottle from the small fridge behind him and handed it over, then pointed at a basket next to the sofa.

"She's hiding. She'll make an appearance if she decides you're worthy. In the meantime, there's bread on the counter. Help yourself. I'll bring dinner out."

I thanked him, then twisted the cap from the water bottle and took a generous sip before rounding the corner in search of the bread. I was ravenous. I bit into the baguette with gusto before turning to check out my surroundings.

Rory's apartment was tiny. Probably half the size of mine and much older. But unlike the rough exterior, it was...pleasant. Surprisingly so. A short wall delineated the narrow kitchen from the main living area. There was just enough room for a sofa, an ottoman, a TV console, and a smallish television. Two barstools were tucked under the small peninsula by the cut-out in the kitchen wall. The palette was basic "dude"...dark leather against stark white walls, though a large red throw rug anchored the room and provided a nice splash of color. It was simple—but tidy and very clean.

"Your place is cool," I commented when he entered the room, carrying two plates and a large bowl.

"Thanks. Let's sit on the sofa. We have more room to eat there," he said decisively as he set his burden on the coffee table. "Help yourself. I'll get some forks, napkins, and extra veggies."

I obeyed and quickly got to work, scooping chicken fettuccine Alfredo onto both plates. Rory joined me a minute later, handing over the silverware before taking a seat next to me. I shot a bashful sideways glance at him as I reached for a napkin.

"Do you eat like this every night?"

"It's really nothing special. I make sauces in bulk and freeze them. Then it's just a matter of adding protein and veggies. By the way, this Alfredo is a healthy version. If you want to drown it in parmesan, feel free. I won't be offended. Cheers." He tapped his water bottle against mine and winked.

"Cheers. And thanks again. This is incredible and very unexpected." I smiled as I twisted the pasta around my fork.

"You're welcome. You sounded anxious, but you said we're cool. Are we?"

"Of course."

Rory tilted his head and shot me a challenging look. "Then kiss me."

"Um...now?"

"Yeah, now. The other night could have been a fluke. Instead of wondering, let's get it over with. One kiss should be enough to tell. C'mere," he commanded, leaning sideways.

I set my fork down and met him halfway until our noses brushed. Then I waited for him to make the next move. He stayed stubbornly still. When I couldn't stand the growing tension, I pressed my lips to his. And wow...amazing.

Rory was a great kisser. He had the simple art of give-and-take down to a science. He molded his mouth to mine and gently pushed his tongue inside. The connection was sweet but bold. It was more about discovery than possession. I hummed as I snaked my arm around his neck, pulling him closer. He sucked my tongue, then bit my bottom lip playfully before pulling back.

"Definitely not a fluke. Eat up, baby, and tell me about your day."

"You don't want to hear about my day," I assured him.

"Sure, I do."

I cleared my throat and willed my heart rate to return to normal before I replied. "It was boring. I had two classes and two practices, and now here I am."

"You sounded frustrated or flustered on the phone. Something happened. What was it?"

"Are you my therapist?"

"If you want me to be," he said around a bite of fettuccine.

I studied his profile thoughtfully. "Okay. Well, I'm up to my eyeballs in stress. Between school, football, my dad's law school campaign, and the new twist in the Max and Sky circus, I can't keep up. It's like I have the world's longest to-do list and five minutes to get everything done. Add you to the mix, and I'm super confused."

"Sounds serious. Let's break it down. Are you struggling in any class besides stats?"

"No."

"Then scratch that off your list. You're going to be fine. I'll make sure of it. Football is your thing, so I doubt it's a worry for you. Your dad might be more complicated, 'cause family is that way. But ask yourself if you'll be happy sitting at a desk in a law firm ten years from now. And remember, it'll be your ass in that chair, not his. If it's not your passion or you just need time to decide if it's what you want, be honest. It's not a crime to have your own dreams. Where was I?"

I stared at him with a dopey grin on my face before refocusing. "Um...Max and Sky."

"Right. What about them?"

I briefly filled him in on my roomie saga as we ate. His incredulous expression was borderline hysterical. He swallowed what was in his mouth before busting into hearty laughter.

"Sounds like a soap opera. Do you think Max jumped in your bed to make his boyfriend jelly?"

I snickered, then dabbed at the corner of my mouth with my napkin. "No, that's not Max's style. He hates being alone. It might be why we didn't make it. We play different sports and we have different schedules and—"

"Whoa. Back up. You and Max were a couple?"

I reached out to smooth the crease at the bridge of his nose impulsively and immediately pulled my hand away. What the hell was wrong with me?

"Yeah. We were together for five years."

Rory gaped. "You're twenty-two! Five years is a fucking eternity at your age! Are you sure this isn't a mind game to win you back?"

"Yeah right," I huffed sarcastically. "Max doesn't know how to play mind games. He also doesn't know how to communicate. And to quote Taylor Swift, we're never getting back together."

"That's very gay," Rory deadpanned.

I chuckled and raised my hand. "Guilty. I'm very gay."

"Good to know. And as your therapist, I have to ask....How do you feel about this gay stuff?"

I regarded Rory for a moment, then picked up a piece of bread before twisting slightly to face him.

"Gay is good," I replied with a lopsided smile.

"Keep going," he prodded.

"I like how I feel when I can be myself. I like it when I don't have to pretend I'm someone I'm not. And I love the sex."

I ripped the bread in half and winked. I noted the lusty slide of Rory's Adam's apple with a perverse sense of satisfaction. I was the world's worst flirt, so I couldn't help feeling proud that I got to him even just a little bit. And yeah, there was something heady about the way he looked at me like I was his new favorite dessert.

Rory let out a ragged sigh as he adjusted himself in his workout shorts. "This Sky dude sounds like he's lashing out. He's insecure in his relationship and with himself, and his family just made it a million times worse by not supporting him. Been there, done that. He's probably questioning his decision, but it gets better after a while."

"Maybe. And good for him if he's ready for it, but I'm not. At least not yet. I shouldn't have to come out on his time clock."

"Of course not," Rory agreed.

"I guess I should be ready for anything. If they split with any animosity whatsoever, I'm gonna get screwed. Sky will make sure the whole damn school knows about the queer quarterback and first baseman who used to be lovers."

"Will anyone really care? Evan paved the way for you last year. Mitch and he were an international sensation. They were getting fan mail from folks on the other side of the world."

"Evan's position wasn't in the spotlight. Mine is...and I'm not ready for the questions and commentary from strangers. It'll be bad enough dealing with my dad when the time comes." I jumped up and paced to the front door and back again. "I just want to graduate. If I can get that piece of paper, I can move on and start over."

"You mean run away," he deadpanned.

"No. That's not running away. It's moving on. It's called growing up."

"Right. Well, eat up. Your food's getting cold."

I scowled at his head when he bent to take a big bite.

"I just told you something kind of significant. You could at least pretend to give a shit," I huffed.

"I give all the shits, Christian. Come sit the fuck down already. You're giving me a crick in my neck," Rory said around a mouthful of pasta.

He patted the cushion next to him in invitation and then motioned me forward meaningfully. I cast my gaze from him to the array of bowls and plates littering the coffee table before closing the distance and flopping down beside him with a heavy sigh.

"Sorry. I told you I'm a mess."

Rory squeezed my thigh. "You're not a mess. But you can only control so much, like the effort you put into your grades or your sport. The rest will work itself out."

"Does that apply to parents too?"

"That I don't know. Everyone's situation is different."

"What did your parents say when you came out?"

Rory went still. He pushed his plate away and leaned forward with one elbow on his knee. "My dad was long gone. But my mom's exact words were 'Get out.' She added a few expletives to make sure I knew how she felt about queers and fucking faggots. Then she held the door open and told me we couldn't talk until I found Jesus."

"Oh. I'm sorry."

"Don't be. Part of the reason I waited so long was that I knew how it would go down. My mom found God when Dad left us. I don't blame her for looking for something to believe in. She had two wild teenage boys, rent to pay, and a nowhere job at a supermarket. She took solace in the bottle for a while, then got sober and tried religion. I want to say it worked for her, but self-righteous misery is a dangerous combo if you ask me. I have no issue with God. I'm a believer. The problem is, I know her God and mine aren't the same.

The messages are too different. One says 'Do unto others as you would have done unto you' and the other adds a clause in tiny writing at the bottom of the page...'but only if they look, act, and share the same beliefs as you.' I prefer the benevolent choice, but maybe that's because I know who I am, and I know I can't change it."

"Who are you?"

"I'm a garden-variety bi guy who really loves dick, baby. I'm not fabulous. I don't like the color pink, but I get turned-on by guys who do. It took me a long time to admit it, but it's liberating. I don't have to pretend anymore. I don't have to lie or evade questions or act like anyone else expects me to. I get to be myself and think about important shit like...getting a fucking job," he said with a laugh.

"Do you think you'll ever talk to your mom again?"

"Maybe. Maybe not. I'm okay either way. I have good people in my life...my brother, my friends. It sucks knowing my mom lives five minutes away and wants nothing to do with me, but I can't lie about who I am to make her comfortable with what she believes."

"Good point."

He shifted to face me so our knees touched. "So we covered school, football, your parents and your ex. Anything else bugging you?"

I shook my head slowly. "Uh...well yeah. Do you really have a cat?"

Rory furrowed his brow in mock annoyance as he slid off the sofa. He crouched on his knees and beckoned the unseen cat forward with kisses and a soft plea to come out of hiding. "C'mere, baby girl. That's a good kitty. Come on, Buttons. There's my pretty girl."

He leaned forward with his hand outstretched and then gently picked her up and cradled her in his arms before presenting her to me. "This is Buttons, queen of this castle, such as it is."

My smile was so wide, it hurt my face. There was something very sweet about this giant of a man holding the small black cat that made my heart flip in my chest.

"She's beautiful." I ran my thumb on top of her head and pet her fur. Buttons purred and licked her white paw nonchalantly as if to say the gesture was acceptable. "How old is she?"

"Five. She belonged to my friend, Cody. He moved to Vermont and couldn't afford to take her with him, so I offered to keep her. She's allowed me the honor for three years now," he said with a half chuckle.

"You're lucky. I've never had a pet."

"Never?"

I snickered at his incredulous expression. "No. I begged my parents for a dog when I was a kid. They gave the old 'We'll see' a million times, but it never happened. When I was seven, I won a couple of goldfish at the fair one year and my dad told me it was a good chance for me to prove I could take care of something. I bought a big fishbowl, blue pebbles for the bottom, an underwater treasure chest, and a mini filter with money I'd been saving in my piggy bank since birth. I read up on how much to feed them, when and how to change their water. I was determined to be the best goldfish owner ever."

"How long did they make it?"

"Forty-eight fucking hours. Can you believe that? I was wrecked. My mom bought me another one 'cause I was so devastated. I think that one lasted a month. Needless to say, I stopped asking for a dog or a cat."

"Dogs and cats are nothing like fish. I bet you could handle it. Here...wanna hold her?"

Rory deposited Buttons into my arms before I could respond, clicking his tongue and cooing softly.

"She's so pretty," I said in an awed tone.

"Wow. I can't believe she didn't bolt. You're good with her."

"I like animals."

"Me too. They're easy. They don't ask for much, and they're always there for you." He leaned in to press a kiss on the cat's head and then mine before standing. "How do you feel about ice cream?"

"I feel really good about it." I grinned.

"Cool. I'll be right back."

Rory gathered our plates and returned a few minutes later with a pint of Ben and Jerry's Chocolate Fudge Brownie and two spoons. Buttons climbed out of my arms with a loud meow when I reached for the ice cream. We chuckled at her obvious annoyance, then settled in and just...talked.

We sat with our legs entwined, passing the container back and forth while we covered religion, politics, the world's best birthday cakes, and our favorite holidays.

"Halloween?" I asked, scraping the bottom of the container before passing it to Rory.

"Yeah. You?" He scowled at the empty pint, then licked the inside edges. I knew it was for comedic purpose, but the sight of his tongue along the rim of that container did things to me.

"Christmas."

"Everyone says that."

I chuckled at his teasing tone. "Are you saying I'm not unique?"

Rory set the empty container on the coffee table. Then he pulled my knee close and absently massaged the inside of my thigh. The gesture was possessive yet tender at the same time. It was a powerful combination that made me want to climb onto his lap and stick my tongue down his throat.

"You're one of a kind."

"So are you," I said, wincing at the note of hero worship in my tone.

Rory's smile widened. He looked like a pirate—sexy as fuck and up to no good. He held my gaze and then tentatively reached out to trace my jawline. I froze. I might have stopped breathing too. It was hard to tell.

He leaned in close enough that I could feel his breath on my lips. He smelled like soap and something woodsy and masculine. I had to taste him again. My awareness of him skyrocketed as we hovered in a sensual standoff. I'd had a crush on him since the first day we met. I thought he was funny, charming, and hot as hell. Now I knew he was smart and kind too. And I knew what it felt like to have him pressed against me in a confined space with his hands on my dick while he devoured me with passionate kisses. I wanted that again. And more.

He caressed my cheek as though we were old lovers with a beautiful story. I leaned into his touch like a cat and let my gaze roam between his eyes and lips. Then I cupped the back of his neck and sealed my mouth over his. I wound my arms around his neck in an effort to get even closer before licking his bottom lip in a wordless request for entry. I could have kissed him all night. I loved the feel of his scruff against my chin and his hand on my lower back. I heard myself whimper when he pulled away to nip at my chin and catch his breath. I didn't want to stop. I raked my fingers down his back and hiked my leg over his intending to push him flat on the sofa.

Rory chuckled lightly as he crooked his hand under my knee, using the momentum to send me backward. Then he climbed over me, crashing his mouth over mine as he rocked his hips rhythmically. His basketball shorts left nothing to the imagination. I could feel his erection through the thin fabric, and just knowing that he was big and thick and that his cum tasted amazing was enough to send me over the edge. I gyrated wantonly in my quest for friction. I wrapped my legs around his waist and my arms over his shoulders, arching my back as we sucked and nibbled each other's tongues and lips. The feverish grinding and roving hands went on for a while, but we both knew there was a point of no return. For me, it might have been a matter of passing out from constricted blood flow. I was so hard, it hurt. I pushed my right hand between us and tried to stealthily unzip my jeans.

Rory froze and then rose above me with a sex-hazed expression that turned me inside out. "Are you sure you want to do that? 'Cause if you take those off, there's a good chance I'm gonna fuck you."

"Oh, my God. Yes." I licked my lips and gulped. "I want you to fuck me. Do you have condoms and—"

"I got everything, baby." Rory stood and offered his hand. "Come with me."

I didn't hesitate. I laced my fingers through his and followed him into a tiny alcove separating his bedroom from the living area. He led me inside the darkened room, pausing to switch the light on. I noted the abstract art poster hanging above the queen-sized bed and the chalkboard next to the closet door. The charcoal-striped duvet and dark-gray blinds on the window were a stark contrast to the white walls. The only real color here was the stack of books on the nightstand. I spotted the title of one on top and then squinted to see if I'd read it correctly. *Astrophysics and Elemental Mathematics.*

My pithy comment about books that doubled as Xanax was forgotten when he set his hand on my hip. The gesture felt familiar and possessive. I liked it. I stepped closer and wrapped my arm around his waist, loving the feel of his thick shaft through our clothes. I rolled my hips to create a little friction and maybe spur him on. It worked. Rory hissed at the contact and pounced.

He covered my mouth, driving his tongue between my lips in a searing kiss that sent me reeling. I slid my hand underneath his T-shirt and splayed my fingers on the small of his back as I angled my head to deepen the connection. We sucked and licked in a frenzy until we were desperate for air. I plucked at the hem of his T-shirt as I stepped back slightly.

"Take it off," I growled.

"You too. Everything."

I nodded and set to work, unbuckling, unbuttoning, and unzipping while he tongue-fucked my mouth with deep, probing kisses. I pushed my jeans over my ass but paused with my fingers hooked under the elastic of my boxer briefs.

"What about you? Go on. I have to see you again."

Rory shot a mischievous, lopsided grin at me, then pulled his tee over his head, revealing the most glorious abs I'd ever seen. His muscular, tatted arms hinted at a beautiful design, but I wasn't prepared for how gorgeous his ink was up close and personal. I wanted to study the detailed angel's wing across his left pec and read the script along his side. But not as much as I wanted to touch him.

He moaned when I traced the writing low on his hip. I glanced down at the tent in his basketball shorts, fully intending to release him and maybe get on my knees and get to work. I lifted my gaze to his eyes to give him what I hoped would pass for a sexy look but stopped midkneel...and gasped.

I straightened immediately and brushed my thumb over the silver bars piercing his nipples. "That is so fucking hot. Does it feel good?"

Rory nodded. "Yeah. My nipples are super sensitive. If I'm wearing a tight shirt and it rubs just the right way...it can be a little dangerous."

I played with the rounded barbells, then bent slightly and flicked my tongue over one and then the other. He hummed his approval, threading his fingers through my hair and massaging my scalp. I slipped my hand under the elastic of his basketball shorts and briefs and cupped his bare ass. Other than the sway of his hips and an occasional yank on my hair, Rory stayed still and let me explore, sucking his tits while I kneaded his bubble butt.

At some point, gravity brought me to my knees. I pulled my shirt over my head, then looked up to meet his gaze before lowering my jeans and briefs just enough to free myself. I loved his crude praise and the lusty grunt of admiration. I just hoped I didn't come too soon when I got my second glimpse of Rory. This was so much nicer than hiding in a closet in a noisy club like a couple of horny teens who couldn't control their libidos. We could take our time here, and I fully intended to do so.

I licked my lips and slowly pushed his shorts down. His dick instantly sprang from the confines and damn, the show just got better and better. Rory was as gorgeous as I remembered. Perfect even. I reached for him automatically and curled my fingers around his thick cock. I brushed my thumb across the wide mushroom head, smearing precum liberally before leaning in to taste him.

"Fuck," he groaned somewhere above me.

That was all the encouragement I needed. I licked the head a couple of times and then traced the prominent vein of his shaft with the tip of my tongue. Up and down, up and down. Then I swallowed him whole. I gagged once or twice before finding my rhythm. Once I did, there was no stopping me. The feel of his hands in my hair and the lusty grunting noise he made while he pumped his hips drove me wild. I fondled his balls with my right hand and rubbed my fingers along the sensitive skin underneath as I stroked myself like mad with my left. When I twisted my wrist and changed my angle, Rory pushed at my forehead.

"Stop."

I held on to the side of the mattress and lost my balance when I tried to stand. He grabbed my elbow to steady me and kissed me hard. Then he pulled back the duvet and told me to sit. I obeyed, shoving my jeans and boxer briefs down my legs and kicking my shoes off while I kept an eye on Rory undressing in front of me. I gripped myself firmly and waited for him to take his socks off and join me, chuckling when he tossed the second one over his shoulder with a flourish. He opened the nightstand drawer, grabbed a bottle of lube and a condom and set them next to me, and motioned for me to scoot back to the middle of the mattress.

"How do you want me?" I asked.

"Anyway I can have you," he quipped, pouring lube into his palm. "That's it. Keep jacking yourself and spread your legs. Wider. Let me look at you. Fuck, that's hot."

I wasn't sure what he was seeing, but my view was spectacular. I never imagined my night would end up here with my naked tutor looming above me, barking porny commands while he massaged the sensitive skin around my hole. He caressed the inside of my thigh sweetly, then bent over to suck my cock as he pressed his finger inside me.

"Oh. Fuck," I groaned loudly.

I arched instinctively to meet his mouth, but when he hooked the single digit and added another, I wanted that too. Rory alternately stroked and licked. I loved the feel of his warm skin and talented fingers. And I loved knowing he was as strung out as I was.

He released my cock and pulled his fingers away before reaching for the condom. Then he rolled it on quickly, and added lube before moving forward and lifting my legs over his shoulders. He held my gaze as he lined himself up with my entrance, pausing to kiss me softly.

"You ready?" he asked.

I nodded and willed myself to relax as he slowly made his way inside me. He stopped a few times to give me a chance to adjust to his girth. He was fucking huge. And though I was more than eager, I was definitely out of practice at being on the receiving end. It hurt. A lot. My muscles tensed and my breathing was short and erratic. Very unsexy. But just when I thought I'd have to tell him this wasn't working, Rory brushed my hair from my damp forehead and kissed my brow, then spoke in a low, soothing voice. He didn't say much, but his gentle chant of "It's okay, I've got you" helped chase my nerves and the last of tendrils of pain away, replacing them with waves of intense pleasure.

I blinked up at him in wonder and threw my arms around his neck. "You feel so fucking good."

"So do you." He trembled slightly as if to keep himself from moving too fast.

"Do it. I'm ready. Fuck me."

Rory growled in response, then captured my mouth as he surged forward. He didn't go too hard or too fast. He simply made every stroke count. Every push and pull of his hips hit the right spot. I lowered my legs, wrapping them around his waist when he picked up speed. But I never stopped kissing him. Our tongues twisted as we met each other thrust for thrust...licking, sucking, and nibbling while we fucked in a growing frenzy. We broke to gasp for air and then did it all over again.

The bed creaked in time with our carnal groans and the sound of our sweat-slicked skin gliding. The rhythmic slap of his balls against my ass was erotic as hell. A tingle of awareness skittered along my spine a moment later. And when he grabbed one of my wrists to hold me still while he slipped his free hand between us and stroked my cock, I knew I wouldn't last.

"I'm gonna—"

Rory bit my bottom lip, then rested his forehead against mine. "Yes. Do it now. Come."

He didn't have to tell me twice. I exploded in a flash of white light. Cum shot over his hand and up my chest. I shook uncontrollably and clung to him like he was the last thing holding me from the edge of a high cliff. Rory pulled me closer when he fell apart a moment later.

We didn't speak for a while, but the quiet felt natural. Until I ruined it with a dreamy sigh that made me sound like a wide-eyed virgin. "Wow."

Dammit. I braced myself for a snarky response designed to keep things real. Something to remind me not to fall for my tutor.

"It was pretty fuckin' 'wow,' wasn't it?"

"Yeah." I grinned, shifting to give him room when he sat up and plucked a few tissues from the box on the nightstand.

Rory dealt with the spent condom on his junk and then leaned over to lick the cum on my stomach before wiping it cleaned. He waggled his brows mischievously then pulled at my arm, wordlessly requesting me to come closer. I sidled next to him and rested my head on his broad chest. He stilled my hand when I tugged at the bar in his right nipple; then he kissed my knuckles sweetly.

"I didn't hurt you, did I?" he asked.

"No, of course not. It was amazing. I admit, I was a little nervous at first. I haven't bottomed in a while."

"How long?"

"Over a year," I replied.

"You haven't had sex in a whole year?"

I snickered at his incredulous expression. "I've done a few things, but not anal. That's kind of a boyfriend thing for me."

"Oh?"

I widened my eyes and shook my head. "No, I'm—I'm not

suggesting we're boyfriends now. I'm just very careful about who I'm with. Max was the last person I was close enough with to trust."

"Hmm. What's the deal with Max and you? How'd you stay besties with the guy you used to fuck?"

I grimaced. "You make it sound so...creepy."

"Serial killers are creepy. Asking about the ex you still live with is just keeping it real."

"Feel free to keep it less real," I snarked. "It's not as sordid as you make it sound."

"From the brief time I met him, I can tell you're just friends, but you gotta admit it's unusual. Can you see me living with Mitch and Evan?"

I chuckled. "No. Evan is very protective of Mitch. He wouldn't share him with you."

Rory furrowed his brow. "Share? Wait. Are you guys a three-some gone bad or something?"

"Fuck, no! Are you nuts? I'm just the ex. It took me a while to move on, but Max and I are better this way. He's restless and reckless. The last few months before Sky came along weren't all that fun. We went from being crazy-in-love high-school sweethearts to college lovers finally living in our own place to...something less."

"What happened?"

"I guess the thrill was over. He got antsy, and then he met Sky. And that was the beginning of the end for us...as a couple. Truthfully, we'd been in trouble for a while. I just didn't want to admit it 'cause I didn't want to lose my friend. We're good at being friends and roommates. Max is a dork who tends to think with his dick, but he's a good guy."

"How long has Sky lived with you?"

"Since July. It hasn't been bad exactly. Just different."

"I couldn't live with my ex and his new guy, even if I didn't want to be with him anymore. I'd plan massive daily pranks to sabotage their relationship. But I'm an asshole like that," he said with a good-natured laugh.

"What kind of pranks?"

"My repertoire is endless. Pick a category...food, bath products, or bedroom antics."

The playful spark in his eyes was hard to resist. I tapped my chin thoughtfully and grinned. "Food."

"Let's see...fill his donuts with mayonnaise. Put toothpaste in his Oreos."

"Ha. Nice try but Sky doesn't eat junk food," I said.

"Fuck, no wonder we hate this guy," he grumbled.

"We don't hate him."

"How do we feel about him?"

"We think he's irritating. But as of this afternoon, there's a concern he's got some misplaced jealousy issues too." I propped myself on my elbow and smiled. "Nicely done."

"What?" he asked innocently.

"I didn't realize you were still playing therapist on me, encouraging me to talk about my feelings. You're tricky...and smart too."

Rory shot a slow-growing grin at me. "I'm very smart."

"I like that about you. Your brain turns me on almost as much as your hot bod. Were you one of those geeky kids in grade school who knew all the answers to every math problem?" I teased.

"Nope. I knew the answers, but I was too nervous to say them out loud. I didn't want to be wrong, so I didn't try. I'm sure my teachers thought I was a classic underachiever from a broken home. It's sad that kids tend to put themselves in boxes defined by others. 'The weird kid,' 'the quiet kid,' 'the brainiac,' 'the jock,' 'the nerd.' In a way, I'm all of those things."

"I know what you mean," I said softly. "Everyone has us

figured out before we do. Then they get insulted when you aren't who they expected."

Rory held my chin and stared into my eyes intently. "Don't let anyone else tell you who you are. That's up to you to decide."

"You're right." I kissed his fingers and smiled.

"So who are you exactly?" he joked.

"A closeted gay quarterback who's scared of what comes next."

"You'll work it out. And if you need anything, I'm here for you." He kept his tone light, but I was touched by his sincerity.

I thanked him, then kissed his nose and his eyelids in a silly attempt to lighten the mood.

"Are you going to teach me everything you know?" I purred, reaching for his half-hard cock.

He pulled me against him and then rolled on top of me. He yanked my arms over my head and rocked his pelvis suggestively, thrusting his cock alongside mine. "Yeah. You're in good hands, baby."

I arched my back and hooked my legs over his ass, humming in approval. "Fuck me again. Please."

Minutes later, when I gripped the sheets with white knuckles as he entered me slowly from behind, I wondered what had taken me so long to give in to this.

Maybe I'd feel a pang of regret later, because surely begging my sexy tutor to fuck me wasn't my best life choice. However, at that moment it seemed pretty fucking inspired. And he seemed like the best thing that had ever come my way.

5

At first, Rory and I stuck to our usual routine. He'd wait for me at our table and greet me with an iced coffee and a roguish smile, but within five minutes we'd be itching for contact. We couldn't keep our hands off each other. Knees under the table, fingers brushing over a homework assignment. It was never enough. I was tempted to give in to his suggestion that we just fuck in the bathroom, but we tended to get vocal during sex and the last thing either of us needed was to guest star on someone's Instagram feed. "Horny QB and tattooed hunk's walk of shame at a local Starbucks." *No thanks.*

After two study sessions, it became apparent that we were torturing ourselves, and I wasn't learning anything new. Rory suggested we meet at his apartment after practice instead. He'd make me dinner and we'd have a private place to study. And have sex. Within a couple of weeks, I was pretty sure we'd fucked on every available surface in his tiny pad. On the sofa, the floor, the coffee table, over the kitchen counter, in the shower, and of course, in bed. I was semi-erect on the drive to his place, and the second he opened the door, it was over. We careened against the walls in a tangle of limbs, clawing at each other's clothes in a quest to get to skin while we licked and sucked on lips and tongues.

There was something special about getting to know a new lover. Rory was the perfect combination of rough and tender. The kind of partner who made sure to cradle your head so it didn't hit the wall when a passionate grinding session heated up faster than expected. He was a big fan of raunchy dirty talk. The naughtier, the better. He loved it when I licked his tits and played with his nipple rings. And he always wanted to know what turned me on. Of course, he had his own style of inquiry. He didn't hold me gently after an intense orgasm and ask if I enjoyed what we'd done. No. Rory was more likely to growl in my ear and demand to know how hard I wanted it. "You want it harder, baby? Say it. Tell me to fuck you harder." I always complied and he more than delivered.

After we cleaned up and redressed, he'd fluff an extra pillow and instruct me to sit before he began our tutoring session. Maybe our methods were unorthodox, but they seemed to be working. I didn't start acing my quizzes right away, but I was definitely getting better. If I kept improving, I'd certainly earn the passing grade I needed. The athletic department would be appeased, and my parents would never know there was ever a doubt. At least, not until my transcript was released to Chilton's law school. But I'd deal with that later.

For now, I was making progress. I hoped.

I shot a wan smile at the professor's assistant when he handed over my most recent quiz at the end of class. I didn't dare look at it yet. Every test was getting progressively harder and though I thought I understood the formulas, I couldn't be sure. I folded the paper, shoved it into my backpack, and walked clear across campus before stopping at a bench under a pepper tree. I took a seat and pulled my cell from my pocket, then mindlessly scrolled through social media until I convinced myself that the scrap of paper burning a hole through my bag was relatively unimportant.

Twenty pics of cute dogs later, I manned up and slipped the test out, folded it open, and...*holy fuck*. I stared at the number on the top right-hand corner as I searched for Rory's name, then pressed Call.

He answered on the first ring. "Hey, how did you—"

"Ninety-eight percent," I blurted.

Silence.

"Really?" he asked, sounding pleasantly surprised.

"Yup. Want me to take a screenshot?"

"No, I believe you. That's awesome. Congratulations. I'm proud of you, baby."

Maybe it was throwaway praise, but I basked in the sentiment like a starving man presented with his first decent meal in months. And yes, I especially loved how easily that last word rolled off his tongue. My cheeks felt suddenly warm to the touch as my goofy grin spread like wildfire across my face.

"Thanks. I think this is a good sign."

"I do too. Were you tired today? You didn't get much sleep last night."

That was an understatement. I fell asleep in his arms and I didn't crawl out of bed until three a.m. Correction, it was four. Rory had pulled me backward, coaxing me with lazy kisses on my neck and along my spine until I lay flat on my stomach. He put a condom on and slowly pushed his way inside. He took his time, speaking in a low, seductive voice about all the things he wanted from me. Mainly, my ass. But that worked for me.

I could still feel him hours later, I mused as I shifted on the bench. "I haven't slept in days, and I'm pretty sure it's your fault."

"My fault? I—hang on a sec." Rory spoke to someone in the background. Something about reps and weight. "Sorry, I'm in the middle of a training session."

"Oh. I'll let you go. Call me later."

"That's okay. Evan doesn't mind if—"

"Evan!" I croaked. "You called me 'baby' in front of Evan. My old teammate? That Evan?"

"Dude. Chill."

"Don't call me 'dude' and don't tell me to 'chill,' " I hissed, pacing the length of the bench and back again.

"Can I tell you to relax? You're blowing up for no reason. I excused myself and walked away. He can't hear me. But even if he could hear, I never said your name."

"Oh. Right." I sighed heavily, then picked up my backpack and flopped gracelessly onto the bench. "Sorry."

"Quit apologizing and go throw a football around or something. Don't you have practice?"

"No. We have a bye this week. Coach gave us the afternoon off."

"Oh. Then come here."

"Where?"

"I'm at the Y. I'm teaching an after-school camp for kiddos, and then I'll be free to teach you."

"No way. I just aced a test and I'd like to rest on my laurels for at least twenty-four hours before I have to come back to earth. So unless you want my company for other reasons..."

"Yeah, I want all those other reasons," he said in a sexy, low voice. "And I want to teach you some wrestling moves too."

I kicked at a pebble next to my foot and frowned. "Excuse me?"

"You heard me. You're wound too tight. Pumping iron or running on a treadmill isn't gonna help. You need to get some of that energy out. I'll text you the address. Traffic might suck right now, but I'll see you within the hour."

"Whoa. I can't wrestle, Rory."

"Not yet, but you can learn. And if it's too hard or you're just not in the mood, we'll take a Zumba class and grab dinner after. What d'ya say?"

I chuckled. "Have you ever taken a Zumba class?"

"Yep. And I'm awesome. But I'm better at wrestling. I gotta go. See you, baby."

He hung up before I could respond. And I wasn't sure I could think that fast anyway. Wrestling? Zumba? Baby? He was probably kidding. Maybe about everything. Rory had an irreverent sense of humor with no real rhyme or reason. He might be teasing me to see what I chose to believe, like it might reveal something about my psyche. He was way more intuitive than I would have thought. But I couldn't figure him out if I didn't try.

Every YMCA I'd ever been to had the same wholesome vibe regardless of the location. A few of my friends used to go to the one in our neighborhood to hang out after school until their parents got home from work. My mom stayed home, so I didn't have a reason to go until I insisted on joining a local basketball league that practiced in the Y's gym. My folks had snobbish views regarding sports. If I was going to play a sport, they would have preferred golf or tennis. I tried those and I was decent enough, but I liked being on a team. There was something satisfying about being part of a system where each person's contribution mattered. Regardless of my skill level, I felt that sense of community every time I stepped onto a basketball court or a baseball or football field. And I felt it the second I walked into the Long Beach YMCA.

I checked in at the front desk with a perky teenage girl with pink hair and a nose ring who gave me a curious once-over when I told her I was there to meet Rory.

"He's finishing up a class in the main gym. You can hang out on the bleachers or wait out here," she said just as a band of wild grade-school kids charged into the reception area, bouncing balls and doing their best to outyell each other.

"I'll wait in the gym."

"Good choice," she agreed with a chuckle.

I made my way down a wide corridor lined with photos and posters commemorating recent events and spotted Rory the second I stepped through the open double doors. He stood in the middle of a series of blue mats laid out on the far end of the area with his hands on his hips. I couldn't hear what he was saying over the echo of activity on my end. A few parents sat in the stands watching their kids' basketball practice. They looked like they might be around six or seven. Rory's group seemed to be a few years older.

They sat at the edge of the mat and appeared to listen intently to whatever he was saying. I wanted to get closer so I could hear him. But when the kids threw their heads back and laughed uproariously to something he said, I felt compelled to observe. I remembered reading somewhere that you could tell a lot about someone by how they treated children and animals. The best teachers were patient, kind, and used inventive measures to hold their pupils' interest. And they weren't afraid to show a silly side to make a point.

So yeah, when Rory suddenly crouched low and did a backward somersault that sent the kids into hysterics, my heart soared. Who could blame me? The badass brainiac was a big ol' teddy bear of a guy with a sweet soul. Fuck, I liked him. A lot. Maybe too much. I hiked my workout bag over my shoulder and made it two steps before someone yanked my elbow and pulled me into a spontaneous hug.

"Hey! What the f—what are you doing here?" Evan asked as he released me.

"I'm...um..." I nodded like an idiot and tried to gather my wits. "How are you?"

"I'm good," he replied.

He looked great, but he always did. Evan was six two with a thick muscular build, dark short hair, brown eyes, and strong even features. He was anyone's definition of a handsome man, but his looks were the least impressive thing about him. He was a good-natured goofball and one of my all-time favorite former teammates. He worked hard but knew how to have fun without being obnoxious or taking advantage of his position. He led by example and he'd always supported me as team captain, whether that meant backing me up in the locker room or attending school functions when he would have rather been home with his boyfriend.

"How's Mitch?"

Evan's eyes lit up. "He's great. He's busy with grad school. Midterms are coming up and he's stressed, but he's doing well," he gushed.

I grinned. "What about you? How's the real estate game?"

"Dude, I'm actually kicking ass. If the market is still hot when you graduate, I highly recommend taking a chance. I bet I can get you an interview at my firm. You interested?"

"I don't know. I have to graduate first...and I've been warned that won't happen unless I pass statistics." I gestured toward the opposite end of the court. "Rory is my tutor."

"He told me. Shocked the hell out of me, that's for sure," he huffed in amusement. "But Mitch always said Rory was really smart."

"He is. He's a math genius." I tried to tone down the note of hero worship in my voice, but Evan's curious double take made me think I was doing a lousy job. "Perez suggested him when I needed help."

"Then you're in good hands." He shot a thoughtful glance in

Rory's direction before turning back to me. "Hey, Mitch and I are having a small barbeque at our house this Saturday. Can you come?"

"Me?" I asked, pointing at my chest like an idiot.

"Yeah, you. I was going to text you anyway. We moved into our new place a couple of weeks ago. It's not perfect yet, but we're getting close. Mitch insisted on buying outdoor patio furniture and a grill last week, so we might as well break 'em in. Nothing crazy. It's a casual get-together with mostly old college friends. Like you. And Rory too. I was just going to remind him about it, but you can do that for me, eh?"

"Uh, sure. So you're friends with Rory."

Evan chuckled. "I know. Weird, isn't it? We bonded over weight training. We spot each other when we lift and talk sports while we run on the treadmills. He's a good guy."

"Mitch doesn't mind that you're friends?"

"Not at all. This is how it went down," he said conversationally. "I joined the Y 'cause I needed an inexpensive place to work out. Day one, I bumped into Rory. I wasn't happy about it. I was all fired up when I got home. Mitch rolled his eyes and told me to grow up and be nice. My plan was to avoid the guy, but the weight room is pretty damn small and Rory is always here. We ignored each other until I almost dropped a barbell on my foot. He saved the day and I guess that broke the ice. We didn't have any big heart-to-heart about Mitch, but he told me he knew we were together and that I'm a lucky guy. That was it. I see him practically every day now. I think Mitch was surprised we became friends, but he's more than cool with it."

"That's good."

"It was Mitch's idea to invite Rory. He thought it would be a nice gesture. There's a decent chance he won't come, but he might if you do."

Warning bells clanged noisily in my head. "What makes you think so?"

Evan shrugged. "He talks about you all the damn time."

"Oh?"

"Don't worry. He doesn't talk about your test scores. He just seems to like you, that's all."

I bit my lip nervously and squinted. I probably looked lost or confused. Both were true. If I didn't snap out of it fast, Evan might get suspicious. Going to a barbeque hosted by old college friends seemed harmless enough, but I didn't know if I trusted myself to be with Rory in public with people who knew us. They might notice something different. I tried not to touch him too often or stare too long, but it wasn't easy.

Everything had changed in the past month. I spent almost all of my free time with Rory. We didn't dance around our attraction anymore. We knew how we felt about each other, and we acted on it constantly. In private, anyway. We didn't hide our friendship in public, but no one knew we were lovers. Well, Max might be curious, but we didn't talk about it. He had his hands full dealing with Sky anyway. They seemed less volatile lately, or maybe that was because I wasn't home as often. We were all operating in a state of willful ignorance, and it worked for now. Maybe it sounded paranoid, but attending a barbeque together might upset the balance.

"I like him too, but I don't think he's going to want to go to a party with me," I bluffed.

"It's hotdogs, hamburgers, and beer, man. It's not a fuckin' date or a—" Evan paused when his phone buzzed in his hand. He glanced at the screen and sighed. "I gotta run. I'm supposed to show a house in fifteen minutes. Listen, I'll text you the time and the address. Mitch said two o'clock...I think."

"Wait! Thanks for the invite, but I'm not sure I can make it," I said quickly.

Evan narrowed his gaze and tapped my forehead with his finger. "I hate to do this, but I gotta pull the guilt card. 'Member all those times in college when you asked me to...and I quote...'do you a favor'?"

I scowled. "Yeah, but—"

"Do *me* a favor and come to the stupid barbeque. And bring a case of beer. See ya, buddy." He patted my shoulder, then headed for the door.

I swiped my hand over my mouth and gulped. Maybe this wasn't a big deal, but it felt like a freak collision of my public and private life. *Fuck.*

I turned toward the action on the mats and laughed aloud at the sight of Rory playing Duck, Duck, Goose with the kids. A skinny boy with wild hair ran around the small circle they'd formed, bopping everyone on the head and calling out "Duck." I sensed the growing buzz of hysteria as Rory prepared to be named "It." He went from a sitting position, then crouched low like a tiger ready to pounce. But his goofy expression was the clincher. The combination of faux serious and silly was slapstick comedy at its finest. The anticipation alone fed the frenzy. So when the boy finally tapped Rory's head, they all hooted merrily and cheered him. He jumped up to chase the kid and pretended to lose his balance to give the boy a chance to make it back to his place in the circle. The kids roared with laughter.

Rory's playful scowl slipped when he noticed me. He glanced at his watch and held up two fingers indicating he was almost free before skipping like a child around the perimeter. I leaned against the wall and grinned as the kids burst into a new round of giggles. They egged him on as he made a second lap.

"It's my turn, Rory!"

"Choose me!"

He slowed down and looked like he was about to stop when someone yelled, "Run, don't skip. That's so gay."

Rory halted midstride and frowned at the kid.

"Well, that's good, 'cause I'm gay," he said matter-of-factly.

I moved away from the wall, casting my gaze from the bleachers to the puzzled-looking kids. Great. Any second now, some irate parent was going to charge forward demanding to know what the hell possessed him to share his private life with their precious darlings. Geez, maybe Coach Perez's kids were out there. I doubted Perez cared if Rory was gay, but he might take exception to a group discussion about it. I wasn't sure what the protocol for defense was in instances like this. Rory wasn't the type of guy to back down from anything or anyone. He wouldn't apologize for stating his truth. And while I admired that about him, I had to admit, it made me very uncomfortable. He was a wild card. Anything could happen.

"You are not," the boy said with a bewildered frown.

"I am," he countered. "Gay people come in all shapes and sizes, and we have all kinds of interests. Just like you. All right. Time's up. See you guys next week. Fist bumps!"

The kids jumped to their feet and surrounded Rory, hopping around him excitedly in an effort to be the first to say good-bye. They seemed unfazed by his revelation, and so did the parents hovering nearby. Rory greeted a few of them before turning to me with a smile.

"How's it goin'?" he asked. "I saw you—"

"Bye, Rory!" A small girl held her hand up for a high five. When he complied, she pointed to me and bit her lip shyly before continuing. "Is he your boyfriend?"

He gave an exaggerated sigh and shook his head. "No. He's just a friend. Don't tell him I have a crush on him."

The girl snickered mischievously, then blurted, "He likes you!"

"Well, I guess that secret is out," he huffed in amusement as he nudged my shoulder. "Come on. Let's get outta here."

Rory motioned for me to follow him out the side door and down a short hallway to a weight-room-slash-mini-gym. There were treadmills and elliptical machines on one end facing a large window with a view of the outdoor basketball court and swimming pool. He greeted a few people but didn't stop until he reached the punching bags positioned over a large swath of mats. I dropped my bag on the floor and took in my surroundings. There were maybe five or six other people working out at the opposite end of the room, but this corner was empty and relatively private.

"This is nice," I commented.

"Yeah, it's not bad. They've done a ton of improvements since I was a kid. This whole section was added on three years ago. We're standing on what used to be the playground. They got rid of the rusty old equipment and replaced it with some swanky new stuff and moved it to the grass by the hoops. Better use of space, if you ask me."

"You came here when you were a kid?" I asked.

"Every day after school." Rory clapped his hands as if to signal a conversation change, then pointed at the punching bags. "Boxing or wrestling? Pick your poison."

"My coach will be pissed if I show up with bloodied knuckles, so wrestling, I guess."

Rory rolled his eyes. "It's not a brick wall, so you'd most likely be fine, but I was thinking we'd try something different and—"

"Hang on." I put my hands up and let out the breath I felt like I'd been holding since he came out to his camp kids in the gymnasium. "What happened back there?"

He frowned. "What do you mean?"

"You told those kids you were gay. Is that gonna be a problem?"

"For who?"

"Don't pretend you don't know what I'm talking about. You came out."

"I *am* out. I don't care who knows. And if an eight-year-old is going to call me gay for skipping, he should know I'm just as gay when I bench press his dad's weight with one hand tied behind my back. It's called a teaching moment, babe. Kids aren't going to learn if they aren't taught. Am I right?"

"Yes. For sure, but...are their parents going to be okay with it?"

"Fuck 'em. I don't care what they think. If they don't want their kids hanging out with me, they can make other arrangements. Any other questions?" he asked sharply.

I licked my lips and nodded. "Yeah, like a million. I thought you just came out a year ago? How did you mentally get here so fast? You don't seem like the type of guy who gives a crap what anyone thinks about him."

"I don't now, but I did in college. I wasn't ready for uncomfortable conversations with my family, friends, or teammates. Everyone assumed I was straight based on looks alone, and it was a helluva lot easier to go along with it. But I was an asshole too. I hinted at being bi in case I got caught in a compromising situation. Then I got really stupid and dated a few girls to back up my claim and appease my mom.

"I was such a dick. I dug holes for myself all over the place. And unfortunately, I wasn't man enough to be in a relationship with an out-and-proud guy who was president of the LGBTQ club and wore pink unicorn shirts every other day.

"Losing Mitch sucked, but looking at myself in the mirror and realizing I was my own worst enemy was even harder. I did some serious soul-searching after a particularly ugly night of excess at a college party. Let me give you a word of advice.... Never try to make a gay man jealous by getting frisky with a girl in his best friend's roommate's bed."

"No shit. You did that?"

"Yeah. I told you, I was jerk. Anyway, the aftermath was my wake-up call. I burned bridges, pissed off some good people, and had to beg forgiveness from Mitch and a really cool girl who, thankfully, is still a friend of mine. And then, I came out. It wasn't pretty, but I did it. My only regret is that I didn't do it sooner."

"Did you do it to win Mitch back?"

"No. He'd already met Evan by then, but that's okay. Evan is perfect for him. They're happy and life goes on. Any other questions?"

"Yeah. Why did you tell that little girl you have a crush on me?"

" 'Cause I do. And the awesome part is, I know you have one on me. Even if you didn't, I'd still like you. You're a cool dude dork. Irresistible combo for me. You're like Clark Kent before he turns in to Superman. If you wore glasses too, I'd be a fuckin' wreck. I betcha I'd walk around with a boner twenty-four seven."

"God, I've been thinking the same thing about you for weeks." I winced the second the words left my mouth. "I mean...'cause you're so smart. Glasses would be a sexy addition. Hot guy with tats and glasses. Geez, just don't tell me you want me to change into one of those wrestler singlet things. I'm half-hard already."

Rory barked a quick laugh and gave me a salacious once-over, lingering on my crotch before making eye contact.

"Since I kinda like my job here, I'm not gonna touch you. Okay...just one little..." He cupped my balls through my workout shorts, then stepped back nonchalantly. He snickered like a kid when I swatted him away and clandestinely adjusted myself.

"Not funny," I hissed.

"Sure, it is." He raised his hands in surrender and sobered. "I know it's not easy, but try not to worry about what everyone thinks, baby."

"I'm assuming you're not talking about touching my junk in public."

"No. I'm talking about letting a kid know I'm gay. I know how it feels to care what everyone else thinks. I used to care way too fucking much. But it's a lot of work, and if you apply simple mathematics, you begin to realize the return ain't worth it."

"Huh?"

Rory squinted, then pointed at my chest. "Nobody is as invested in your life as you. Period. Not your mom, your dad, or best fuckin' friend. Nobody else walks in your shoes or sees through your eyes or feels what you do. Even when they want to, they can't. So why should I care if Joey's mommy and daddy are pissed I told their kid I'm gay? I'm not teaching sex ed here. I'm stating a fact. My eyes are blue, the sky is blue, the locker room smells like dirty gym socks....I'm bi. I said gay instead of bi to avoid a lengthy discussion with an eight-year-old, but the way I see it is, I told the truth. Nothing fancy about it. No hidden agenda. I'm not starting a club and recruiting new members. I'm only keeping it real for myself."

I held his stare. Sure, I agreed with the sentiment and I respected his viewpoint. But I didn't want to engage in a "coming-out" conversation when all I could say was, "I'm scared," or "I'm not ready." It sounded cowardly and weak. I thought I was better than that, but maybe I wasn't.

I gestured toward the mats when I couldn't think of anything to say.

"So what are we doing here?"

"Wrestling, remember?"

"Um...I don't wrestle. And even if I did, neither of us is dressed for it."

Rory's gaze roamed over my basic black workout shorts and

white tee. He lingered on my crotch for a moment, then glanced down at his similar ensemble with a grin. His shorts were dark gray, but his shirt matched his eyes and—fuck, he was sexy.

"We aren't doing anything crazy. I might cop a feel, but I promise I won't yank your shorts down." He paused before adding, "Unless you want me to."

I hooked my thumb toward the occupied machines. "I do, but we aren't alone. Why don't we lift weights or jump on a treadmill?"

" 'Cause that's boring."

"And wrestling isn't?"

Rory gasped theatrically. "Spoken like a true football snob."

I chuckled. "I'm not a football snob. Well, maybe a little, but I like other sports too."

"Name your top five."

"Football, baseball, hockey, basketball, and soccer. What about you?"

"Wrestling, boxing, tennis, curling—what are you laughin' at?" he asked with a faux scowl.

"No one says curling."

"Well, they should. It's awesome."

"Pushing a rock on ice is slightly less than awesome," I snarked.

"Hmph. Some might say the same about throwing a ball up a field and getting tackled," he countered.

"Millions of fans would disagree with your sarcasm."

Rory huffed. "Yeah, well, just because something is popular doesn't make it good."

I gasped in faux outrage. "I'm sorry, did you bring me here to trash my sport?"

"No, I wanted an excuse to roll around on top of you," he deadpanned. "And I think we should place a side bet to see who gets hard first." He held up his forefinger and grinned. "Let's make this interesting. Whoever pops a boner first has to do whatever the winner says."

"No way. I'll be the one who gets arrested for public indecency and that will *not* be my 'coming-out' story," I assured him haughtily.

"When the time comes, I can't wait to hear your story. But don't worry...I expect better than an X-rated wrestling match. We'll be discreet. When I win, I won't jump up and down and point at the flagpole between your legs." He winked before clapping and taking a step backward. "You ready?"

"Okay, but what are the rules?" I squatted with my hands on my knees the way I might if I was at the line of scrimmage on a football field waiting for the ref to blow the whistle.

"My boy likes rules," Rory said with a grin.

I lifted an eyebrow in amusement. "Your boy?"

"Yeah. You're mine. Don't argue."

I held his gaze for a long moment and then smiled. "Okay."

"The first person to pin their opponent to the mat is the winner. In a real match, you can earn points for either taking me down or escaping my hold if I take you down first. And not to get too technical here, but there are penalty points too. Same idea as football. No unnecessary roughness, no grabbing clothes, leaving the mat, delaying the match. It's all pretty standard."

I straightened and gave him a serious look. "Got it, but you have to watch out for my shoulder and don't touch my right hand. You're strong and I can't get hurt."

"Christian, I'm not going to hurt you. That's not the idea. It's exercise. Energy release. It might not be your way, but I wanted to show you this because it's always helped me."

"How?"

"I can tell you're stalling again, but I'll play along," Rory said with an exaggerated sigh. "I had ADHD and probably a few other things that didn't get picked up when I was a kid...food allergies, social anxiety, and I couldn't sit still. You name it, I had it. A doctor eventually prescribed drugs that were supposed to help my concentration. The medication sort of worked, but it was expensive and when my mom couldn't afford it anymore, one of the counselors here suggested diet and exercise changes. Justin and I were regulars at the after-school program already. They knew us pretty well, and no one was surprised I didn't do as well at team sports. In a weird way, I'm a perfectionist and I couldn't handle not being in charge." Rory paused and gave me a quirky grin. "Kinda like you."

"Ha. Ha. So that's when you found wrestling?"

"Yeah. Not immediately. I tried karate, boxing, tennis, but I liked wrestling best. There was a class here every day, and wait for it...I had a wicked crush on one of the student instructors," Rory admitted with a laugh.

I smiled. "How old were you?"

"Fourteen, I think. His name was Nelson. He was tall but kinda thick with brown hair, brown eyes. He wasn't super hot or anything, but he was nice and very patient."

"Was he your first boyfriend?"

"No. He was straight as an arrow. It was a completely platonic relationship." Rory squinted and gave me a funny look. "And now I have no idea why I told you all that. Probably 'cause you're always asking me personal questions."

"I am not!"

"Sure you do. Which was your first tattoo? Are you gonna pierce your cock? What are you making for dinner tonight? Geez, it's like I'm under a magnifying glass," he griped good-naturedly.

I threw my head back and laughed hard enough to attract a few curious glances. "Those are *not* personal questions. Well, maybe the piercing one is, but..." I furrowed my brow and set my hands on my hips. "Are you really going to pierce your dick?"

"Fuck, no!" He snorted. "But that's not the point."

"What *is* the point?"

"Honestly, I don't remember. I was going for a correlation between our sports. Offense versus defense. A quarterback plays the lead offensive position in football. You're almost never on defense. In wrestling, you're on your own, just like in real life. You've got to play both sides all the time. And correct me if I'm wrong, but it seems to me that you play offense on the field and defense in real life." Rory paused to gauge my reaction to his very astute observation. When I didn't argue, he continued. "In wrestling, you fight like crazy to get some asshole off of you and the next, you're on top. Your opponent knows without seeing your face that you call the shots. He can feel your strength and energy and he can probably feel your dick too."

"Nice visual," I replied sarcastically.

"I know, right? Maybe that didn't make sense. Let me show you." He pointed at the opposite corner of the mat. "You stand over there. We start in neutral across from each other, one foot on the mat, the other off. That's right. The idea is to stay in bounds or for our purposes, on the mats. There's a host of basic rules, but let's stick with common-courtesy ones. No scratching, pulling hair or clothes, or biting."

"I can't bite you?"

"No, wise guy. And remember...offense. Ready?"

I nodded and took a step forward just as Rory charged at me. He picked me up around my middle and flattened his chest over mine. He pulled my arms above my head, then leaned down and bit my bottom lip. "I win."

I curled my legs around his upper right thigh and tilted my hips so my half-hard prick grazed against his as I shifted my weight. I hoped to throw him off guard and use momentum to topple him sideways, but he was too big. And honestly, I loved the feel of his weight on me.

I should have been mortified at my body's traitorous response to him. I didn't care who was watching. I wanted him to yank my shorts down and drive his cock inside me. I wondered if there was a way to fuck in the corner of a gym while everyone else went on with their conversations, completely oblivious to the live porn unfolding on the mat. It would be like something from a perverted dream. Me and the coach, the tutor, my tattooed wrestling opponent with the sexy smile and the beautiful eyes.

"Damn, I want you to fuck me, Rory," I whispered, licking the shell of his ear.

He gave me a puzzled look as he rose above me, holding my wrists to keep me still. "What are you doing?"

"Nothing. I was just thinking this is hot. I can feel your cock through your shorts. I want to slip my hand inside and squeeze your balls and—"

Rory set his hand over my mouth and widened his eyes comically. "Whatever you're doing, stop."

I lowered my eyelashes and went completely still in a gesture I hoped he read as contrite. The second he pulled his hand away, I bit the side of his palm and shoved his chest hard and pounced. The element of surprise gave me the advantage. When he fell sideways, I dove on top of him and sealed my mouth over his. This was a bigger deal than he probably guessed. I'd never kissed a man in a public space that wasn't completely LGBTQ-friendly. Ever.

I licked his lips and slid my tongue inside, threading my fingers through his hair as I deepened the connection. Then I smacked the mat underneath him three times before breaking the kiss with a grin.

"I won." I taunted.

Rory snorted in amusement and pushed me. I sat beside him with a big-ass smile on my face, knitting my legs together to hide my erection.

"You're a sneaky brat and you know I can't retaliate, or I'll end up fucking you on this mat."

I waggled my eyebrows. "So admit it...I won. Go on. Say the words. 'Nice job, Christian. You kicked my ass.' "

"Ha. You cheated and basically racked up a shit-ton of penalty points. If this was a real match—"

"I would have won," I intercepted, nudging his shoulder playfully.

"You would have been disqualified. In a football game, you'd have been ejected."

"Ejaculated?"

Rory shot a stern look at me. "Whatsa matter with you? You look drunk or high or something."

I snickered. "Nope. I'm just happy 'cause I—"

"You did not win so don't say it." He glowered as he shifted to stand. "Come on. Let's try it again."

I pulled his elbow so he fell beside me. "That's not what I was going to say. Did you notice that I kissed you? In public."

Rory cocked his head and squinted before turning toward the other patrons on the far end of the room. "This barely qualifies as 'public.' And what's up with you anyway? One second you're freaked out that I told a kid I'm gay and the next, you turn into a sex fiend in front of the treadmill crew."

I chuckled appreciatively and leaned back, bracing my weight on my hands as I took in his handsome profile. "Sorry. I guess I got carried away."

"Don't apologize. It feels good out of that closet, doesn't it?" When I opened my mouth to reply, he set his finger over my lips. Then he hopped to his feet and extended his right hand to help me up. "That was a rhetorical question. No answer required."

"Evan invited me to his house for the barbeque he told you

about this weekend," I blurted. "He suggested we go together and...let's do it. Do you want to go with me?"

"Are you asking me on a date?"

I pursed my lips and nodded. "I am. We don't have to hold hands or anything crazy, but maybe that's okay too. I'm just willing to try...if you're cool with it."

Rory looked like he was waiting for a punch line. His mouth was set and his eyes didn't give anything away. After twenty minutes...or two seconds, he inclined his head and grinned.

"I'm cool with it."

I snickered at the funny face he made, and when it bubbled into something that felt like joyful release, I let go and laughed aloud. A date. I hadn't planned on that at all. But it suddenly seemed like a great idea. Evan and Mitch's friends were mostly recent graduates from Long Beach State, and they were a very gay-friendly crowd. We didn't have to make any grand announcements. We didn't have to say a word. But if he stood a little closer than usual and set his hand on my lower back, the way he sometimes did when no one was looking, I wouldn't pull away. Not this time.

The twelve-pack of beer tucked under my arm weighed a ton. I felt like I was dragging an anvil up a mountain in the snow. I glanced at Evan and Mitch's house from the sidewalk and gave myself a pep talk as we made our way to their front door—the way I might if in a huddle. This was my personal "fourth down with a yard to go at the goal line." I could do this. And if I needed help, the guy next to me was willing to jump in. We'd talked about strategic exit plans on the way over.

"We need a signal," Rory suggested, lifting his right hand from his steering wheel. "How 'bout a peace sign?"

"Sure, but what for?"

"I don't know. If you feel nervous or just jumpy and you want someone close...I'll be there."

I twisted in my seat and studied his profile. A wave of adoration and affection hit me so hard, I lost my breath for a moment. Fuck, I loved him. No...wait. I didn't love him. I couldn't. It was too soon. We'd only known each other a couple of months. It wasn't possible to feel this much for someone so fast. Or was it?

I grabbed his wrist and kissed his hand. I wanted to tell him how I felt right then and there, but I didn't know how to say, "I want you so much, I can't breathe sometimes." So I nodded instead. "Yeah, a peace sign is a good idea. But it'll be fine. I've met most of Evan's and Mitch's friends at other parties. They're all cool."

"So are you. And we don't have to stay long," he assured me. "Let's just eat a hamburger, drink a beer, and then go back to my place and play with Buttons."

I kissed his hand again, then bit his thumb, chuckling when he pulled away, shaking his wrist. "Hey, Rory?"

"Yeah?"

"I like you a lot. Like...a lot, a lot," I confessed with my heart in my throat.

He pulled up to the curb down the street from Mitch and Evan's, then turned to me with a blinding smile. "Same, baby. Let's do this."

I heaved the beer from the floor of his pickup truck and happily walked by his side, kicking the autumn leaves along the path like a school kid. But as we approached the quaint gray bungalow on the quiet residential street, my nerves returned full force. Rory was right about me. I played defense in real life. I let circumstances dictate my actions instead of taking control the way I would on the field. I wasn't a total pushover, but I wasn't in command the way I was in a game.

Before I could mentally berate myself for being weak or lame, Rory hooked his finger in my belt loop and tugged. "You okay?"

"Yeah."

He gave me a reassuring smile and flashed a peace sign. I bit the inside of my cheek and nodded just as the door swung open.

Mitch pulled me inside and hugged me impulsively.

"You're here! Come on in. Everyone is out back. We totally lucked out with the weather. You never know what it'll be like in the middle of November."

Mitch was five eleven, tops, with short blond hair, pretty blue eyes, and sharp features. He had elegant, effeminate mannerisms for sure, but he was tough as hell. I'd been as shocked as everyone else when Evan came out last year and introduced Mitch as his boyfriend. First of all, I had no clue Evan was bi and second, I wouldn't have guessed Mitch would be his type. But they seemed to complement one another well, and they were obviously head over heels for each other.

Even though I knew they were ancient history, I tried to picture Mitch with Rory. And I just couldn't do it. They didn't fit. Rory was mine.

"Right," I agreed as Mitch turned to greet Rory with a warm smile and brief embrace.

I watched them carefully, looking for signs of longing or regret, but the hug was over before it began, and Rory was at my side a second later. He snatched the case of beer from me and asked our host where he wanted it.

"Evan put the cooler outside. We're still waiting on a couple of people before we start grilling, but Derek and Gabe and Chelsea are here and..."

Mitch walked ahead of us, giving a breakdown of the guest list as he headed through the living room to the adjoining kitchen and the wide, sliding glass door leading outside. The house was tastefully decorated with midcentury modern touches and bright colors I knew were all Mitch. On a good day, Evan was happy his socks matched, I mused as we stepped onto the wood deck.

I scanned the yard for familiar faces. Mitch's best friend, Chelsea, was chatting with a couple of girls at the outdoor table under a red umbrella. I spotted Evan's friend, Derek and his boyfriend, Gabe, near the grill, talking to Evan. There were a few others I didn't know but sort of recognized from previous get-togethers. I had an automatic sense of being in friendly territory with good people. Everyone was roughly my age or a couple of years older, going through similar experiences, navigating the final year of college, or embarking on life as a recent graduate. I was suddenly very glad to be there.

Rory headed for the grill and greeted Evan with a one-armed bro hug. He stepped aside to give me room to do the same, then handed the case of beer to Mitch.

"I'll put these in the cooler and bring you cold ones," Mitch said. "Anyone else need another?"

"I do. Thanks, baby." Evan gave his empty bottle to his boyfriend as he drew him against his side and kissed his cheek.

"No, we just got one. Thanks," Derek said, lifting his beer bottle as proof before turning to me with a smile. "How's it goin', man?"

"Good. What are you guys up to these days?" I asked, casting my gaze between Derek and Gabe.

They were a hot couple. No other way to say it. They'd met on the water polo team at Long Beach State. They were both tall and lean with toned swimmers' physiques. Derek looked like a typical California kid with blond hair and golden skin, while Gabe had dark hair and eyes and olive skin. They came out last year, just days before Evan. It was a mind-blowing week, for sure. But now, it seemed so natural. Derek and Gabe fit, the same way Mitch and Evan did.

"I'm a couple of months into culinary school and I'm working at that new French bistro on 2nd Street. It's insanely busy, but I love it," Derek said with a wide grin before snaking his arm around Gabe's waist. "And this guy is still studying for exams, like you."

Gabe groaned. "I'm so over the school part. I'm glad I took five years to get it all done, but it'll be nice to graduate next spring and spend more time in the pool."

"How's the Olympic training going?" Rory asked.

"Great," Gabe replied enthusiastically before launching into a rundown of his daily workouts with the national squad and his chances for winning a place on the team at the next summer Olympics.

We stood in an easy circle for a while, catching up and commiserating about transitioning into grown-up mode.

"Finding a job I actually want is harder than I thought. I got an offer from a finance company in LA last week. The money is great but I'm not ready to have my soul sucked from my body just yet," Rory groused.

"You didn't tell me," I said softly.

"I know. I just...wanted to think about it first."

Gabe, Derek, and Evan shuffled to make room for Mitch when he joined our circle. Rory and I stood closer now, kind of like the others were, except they were established couples. I wondered if Mitch knew something was up. He cast a curious look between us as he handed us beers. Then he cuddled up to Evan and rested his head on his boyfriend's shoulder.

"What do you want to do?" Mitch asked.

"I think I want to teach," Rory replied right away.

"You do?" I cocked my head curiously.

"Yeah. I looked up the info on certifications for substitute teaching. I want to see if I like it before I apply to graduate school, but...yeah, I think I might be good at it."

I nodded in agreement, then impulsively hugged him. "You'd be amazing. Really fucking amazing."

Rory slipped his arm around me and returned my smile. He didn't say anything, but he didn't have to. The silent communication was more than enough. It voiced pride, appreciation, encouragement, and yes...affection. And everyone in that circle knew it.

Was I out now? Did I care? I hadn't intended to come out necessarily, but this felt right somehow. No one here would judge us. This might be a perfect place to admit I had more in common with these guys than friendship, age, and athleticism.

"I'm gay," I blurted in a decidedly uncool rush. "Weird timing, I know, but I figured I could tell you guys and, um...yeah."

My announcement was met with surprised silence, then a celebratory whoop and a round of high fives, hugs, and congrats. We earned a few curious glances from the opposite end of the yard, but no one jumped up to see what the fuss was about. And I immediately realized I wanted to keep it that way for now. I mentioned it to my friends.

"No worries, Christian. Take your time," Mitch said with an indulgent grin.

"I gotta say, I'm surprised, but...you two sort of fit. How long have you been together?" Evan asked.

"Um, it's recent," I replied vaguely.

"Gotcha." Evan patted my shoulder, then slugged Rory's bicep in a show of bro affection before declaring he needed to start grilling.

When our little group dispersed, Rory pulled me under an overgrown lemon tree partially hidden from the house. He glanced over his shoulder to see if anyone was looking before backing me against the trunk. Then he held my face, caressing my cheeks with his thumbs before leaning in to press his lips to mine.

I blinked when he pulled away. Stars and fireworks danced in my periphery. I felt alive and free and part of everything around me in a way I never had. Because of Rory. I wasn't sure how to thank him, though, or if it was even appropriate. So I stared at him like an idiot and pulled him close, so he rested his forehead on mine.

"Did you mean to do that?" he whispered.

"No. But it felt good. Freeing. You know, that's only the second time I've ever said those words out loud."

"Say it again."

"I'm gay."

"I'm glad." Rory kissed my nose and then my lips. "Very glad."

"When were you going to tell me you decided to teach?"

"Tonight, tomorrow...I don't know. It's something I've been thinking about for a while."

"You're a natural. You're patient and fun, but you don't take any shit. And you're the smartest guy I've ever met," I gushed.

"Aww, now why do I think you're trying to get in my pants?"

I chuckled as I looped my arms over his shoulders. " 'Cause I am. Want to know something crazy?"

"Mmmhmm."

"I want to be like you when I grow up. Except I want to coach."

Rory pulled back and squinted as if to see if I was serious. "Really?"

"Yes. I love football. I can't play forever, but I want to find a way to stay on the field."

"Then do it. You can be anything you want to be, Christian. No limits, no boxes. If you want it, go for it."

I nodded thoughtfully then bit the inside of my cheek. "I want you."

Rory flashed a devilish grin, then sealed his mouth over mine and pushed his tongue between my lips. We made out against the tree until a roar of laughter from the house spilled outside, reminding us that we weren't alone.

"I want you so fucking bad right now. Do you think anyone would notice if we disappeared?" he whispered, biting my bottom lip.

"I don't care. Let's go."

He kissed me roughly, then grabbed my wrist and set my palm over his jean-clad erection before lacing our fingers. I didn't pull away. I was lightheaded and dizzy, and it felt almost necessary to have some kind of physical connection to him. We made our way toward the house, hand in hand. No one seemed to notice us. Derek, Gabe, and Mitch were talking to Chelsea and her friends now while Evan manned the grill. His gaze was locked on whatever he was cooking, but I could see his lips move as he chatted with the huge man standing beside him.

The bigger man guffawed at something Evan said. He turned slightly as though needing space to compose himself and that was when he noticed me. He waved a greeting, then opened his mouth and immediately closed it just as I dropped Rory's hand.

"Jonesie. Hey...um, when did you get here?" Lame. Like totally embarrassingly lame. Thank God for the longer autumn shadows. I hoped like hell they hid my blush.

"Uh...now. Or five minutes ago, I—" He looked from me to Rory and back again with wide-eyed shock. Then he stuck his right hand out and introduced himself to Rory. "I'm Taylor. Um, Taylor Jones. I play ball with Christian. Offensive tackle."

Rory shook Jonesie's hand. They exchanged a round of awkward pleasantries while I stood silently in panic mode. My head whirled in a gazillion directions. Did he see? Of course, he did. Should I tell him not to say anything or was it understood? And did I know his first name was Taylor?

"Burger or hotdog, Rafferty?" Evan asked, breaking my reverie.

"Um, I think we're gonna go," I choked.

"There's no need. Jonesie's cool." Evan furrowed his impressive brow and glared at the bigger man. "Aren't you?"

Jonesie stuffed his hands into his pockets and nodded profusely. "Of course."

I held his gaze for a long moment. Jonesie seemed sincere,

but he was also in some state of shock. He couldn't stop staring and fidgeting. Processing my gayness was more than he'd bargained for at a friendly backyard barbeque. I almost felt sorry for the guy. But I didn't want to hang around to discuss it with him either. I inclined my head in acknowledgment, then thanked Evan before turning back to my teammate.

"See you Monday."

I tried to act as casual as possible as we said our good-byes. I felt like I was on the field, setting up a play while I sized up our biggest threat. Obviously, Jonesie was the threat, but in a strange twist, I trusted him. He'd done battle for me for years as a defensive guard and now on offense. He was the last guy between me and our opponent, and he'd never let me down. I didn't think he would now either.

RORY KNEW ME WELL ALREADY. He sensed my anxiety, but he didn't push me to talk about it. He put some eighties music on in his truck and sang to me all the way back to his place. He held my hand as he led me to his room. And he made love to me. Every part of me. He sucked my cock until I was about to explode. Then he entered me slowly, moving with a sweetness that made me weak in the knees. He took me over completely, encouraging me to open up and let him in.

I hitched my legs over his shoulders and clutched his ass, begging for more. He rolled his hips seductively and picked up the pace.

"You like that, baby?"

"Oh fuck, yes. Harder," I groaned.

Rory delivered. He yanked my hands above my head and thrust inside me over and over. The rhythmic thump of bedsprings and the sound of our bodies colliding permeated the air. I was on the verge of orgasm. My cock was painfully hard already. One or two strokes would be enough to send me over the edge. But I couldn't slip my hand between us to stroke myself without messing with his tempo. When he sensed what I was trying to do, he went still and then pulled away and lay on his back.

"Get on top of me."

I scrambled to obey him. I straddled his torso and lowered myself onto his thick cock. I braced both hands on his chest and met his gaze. Then I rocked forward and backward to test the new position.

"This is good. I love the way you feel inside me." I grunted when Rory arched his back and grabbed my dick. I sighed happily, tugging gently at his nipple bars until he made a whimpering noise that made me feel like a fucking god.

"Get movin'. I'm seconds away from coming in your ass."

"Oh God, that's hot. I want that. No condoms. I want to feel your cum. I want you to feel mine too. Will you let me fuck you?"

"Fuck, I'm gonna come," Rory growled. He pumped his hips upward and slapped my ass hard with his left hand while stroking me with his right.

The combination of his hands, his dick, and the dirty talk was sensory overload. I fell apart seconds later. Rory pulled me over him, then rolled over so he was back on top. He drove inside me over and over until we both stopped shaking.

It took a while to come back to earth. Personally, I was content to live in the clouds for as long as possible. Real life had a way of killing the fun. Rory obviously felt the same way. He set his finger over his mouth and led me to the bathroom. We washed each other, then dried off, hurried back to bed, and lay quietly entwined under the covers until an insistent meow broke the silence.

"Buttons must be hungry," I murmured.

"Mmm. I'll feed her and bring us a snack too. Stay here." Rory kissed my forehead and padded into the living area.

I grinned at the melodic tone he used to talk to his cat. "How's my pretty girl? Are you hungry? What kind of cat delicacies are we serving up tonight?"

His syrupy inquiries were met with meows. It was part of his daily routine. He talked to her constantly, and I had to admit the sweetness melted me every time. He rolled his eyes at my sappy smile when he returned to the room holding two bags of chips.

"I'm starving. I'll make stir fry or something in a bit, but these will do for now. Which ones do you want, the blue Hawaiian chips or the Lay's original?"

"Yum. I love Hawaiian chips," I said, propping my pillow against the wall and drawing the striped duvet around my waist.

Rory made a face as he popped the bag open and handed it to me. "Better blue chips than blue balls, I guess."

My chuckle turned to a moan when he reached between my legs. I tilted my hips to meet his touch, marveling that I felt even a glimmer of desire after what we'd just done. I loved that he didn't hold back. I was dying to know if he'd left a handprint when he spanked me before he came. My ass ached. In fact, I was sore all over. But it felt amazing.

"I can't believe I'm getting hard again." I swatted his hand away and pointed to the textbook on the nightstand. "Either tell me your favorite snack or bore me with math. We can't do it again."

Rory snickered. "Don't worry. My dick is gonna fall off if I don't give it a rest. As far as snacks go, I like peanut butter on almost anything. Celery, pretzels...hell, I'm happy eating it straight out of the jar."

"Mmm. I do that sometimes too. Just get a big spoonful and throw a couple of chocolate chips in. Delish. It's the homemade desperado version of Reese's Peanut Butter Cups."

"It's good on potato chips too."

I shot him a dubious sideways glance. "Seems like a stretch."

"Baby, I'd put peanut butter on anything and eat it. Including your ass. Correction...especially your ass. Roll over and let me look at it," he replied, making a circular motion with his hand.

I shook my head. "No way. I'm too sore."

"What part of 'My dick is about to fall off' sounds like I'm ready for round two?" he snarked. When I still didn't budge, he caressed my upper thigh and brushed a strand of hair from my eyes. "No monkey business. I promise. I just want to make sure you're okay. Lie on your stomach."

I heaved a dramatic sigh before setting the bag of chips aside and obeying. "I'm fine."

Rory leaned over to grab a bottle of ointment from his night-stand drawer, then climbed over me and straddled my legs. "I've been there too a few times and—"

I twisted under him and glanced up in surprise. "Really? I didn't think you bottomed. So when I said I wanted to be inside you..."

"The answer is yes." He winked before squeezing the gel on his palm. "This should feel good. Relax. That's it."

I flinched at first but his fingers were magic. Or maybe it was the deep timbre of his voice. My mind ricocheted around twenty topics at once. Every thought centered on the delicious hunk rubbing ointment on the sensitive skin around my entrance. *He said he'd bottom. He said he liked peanut butter. He smells so good.* Oh yeah, and one other thing...*I came out tonight.*

"I feel like we should talk," I said softly.

"Go on. I'm listening."

"Well, it's kinda awkward with your fingers in my ass."

Rory pressed kisses along my spine, then nuzzled my neck. "Hold that thought. I'm gonna wash my hands."

I waited for him to return to bed and settle beside me before setting a potato chip against his lower lip. "You know, I didn't mean to tell them about me tonight. It felt like a huge achievement until Jonesie walked in."

"Do you think he'll out you?" he asked around a mouthful of chips.

I furrowed my brow. "Not intentionally. He's not malicious. He rallied around Evan the second he came out. But it might be different with me."

"How?"

"I'm team captain. I'm the leader. Evan was a fifth-year senior at the end of his final season."

"Other than job title, it sounds like your timing would be roughly the same. I mean, if you decided to come out all the way."

"Yeah. You know, I've been thinking about my future a lot lately, and it feels like my focus has been about what I don't want. I don't want to go to law school, I don't want to live with Max and Sky, and I don't want anyone to know who I really am. It's like you said...I'm on defense twenty-four seven, and it's fucking exhausting. But if I turn it around and ask myself what I want, my perspective changes in a good way."

"So what do you want?"

"I want football. I want to make a career of it somehow. My dream job would be Offensive Coordinator for an NFL team. I don't know the path exactly, but I can figure it out. And I want to stay on at Chilton one more year. I've got another season in me for sure. I love the game. Why walk away now?"

"I like this plan," Rory said with a toothy grin.

"Me too. My dad will flip. He's not going to be willing to pay for a fifth year so I can minor in kinesiology and physical education. I'll have to take out a student loan. That's okay. It'll be worth it. The tricky part is coming out. I always thought I'd wait until I graduate, but now...I don't know."

Rory sat up and gave a thoughtful once-over. "You don't have to do it all at once, baby. We can stay on the DL until next year. Take your time. I'll give you all the room you need to figure it out. I'm your tutor. We've a reason to be together, and we'll make it work for as long as we can."

I frowned. "What does 'as long as we can' mean?"

"I'm a 'what you see is what you get' kind of guy. You never have to worry about me not being honest with you. I know how the partial in-and-out-of-the-closet scenario goes. You never really have to commit. You let people think what they want while you go about your business. In theory, that's fine. The truth is, there's always an unaccounted variable that skews the whole equation and creates a—"

"Whoa. Stop." I set my hand over his mouth and narrowed my gaze. "Why are you talking 'math language'?"

"Am I?"

"You are. What's wrong?"

"Nothing. I'm just trying to tell you that I'm not gonna stand in your way. I want to see you tackle your dreams head on. I wanna see you on offense. And I don't ever want to be the reason you didn't go for it one hundred and ten percent. Does that make sense?"

"Sort of, but it sounds like you're giving yourself an out."

"It's the other way around, Christian." He bent to kiss my temple before getting out of bed and heading for his dresser. He stepped into a pair of gray sweatpants that hung low on his hips, then grabbed the bags of chips. "We gotta eat real food. I'll start chopping veggies. Do me a favor and strip the sheets off the bed. We don't want to sleep in crumbs tonight."

I stared after him for a long moment, mulling over his ability to make a major statement using a mere six words. He was right. I was the one with the escape route. He was out and proud, and I was contemplating whom I could trust with something I'd known about myself for over a decade. And then he'd called me by my name to emphasize his point. He rarely called me Christian. I was QB or babe or baby. The separation between formal and familiar...who we were in the beginning versus who were now. This version of us could only last so long if we weren't committed and honest about who we were to each other.

The future I envisioned included the hunk singing to his cat in the kitchen. I didn't want the short-term fix. I wanted forever. And that would require a big statement and some big fucking balls. I'd always considered myself to be reasonably brave, but I was beginning to realize I'd never really been tested.

Something told me that was about to change.

I WAS RIGHT.

Max texted me Monday afternoon before practice. *Sky moved out. Call me.*

I studied the message for a second, then checked the time. *I have ten minutes to get dressed and on the field*, I thought before pressing Call.

"Moved out?" I asked when he answered on the first ring.

"He cleared out his stuff. Everything's gone. His clothes, his shoes, his flavored condom collection. Everything."

"Okay. This is sudden." I leaned against the stucco wall to get out of the breezeway. The cold November wind carried a serious bite. "Or did you know?"

"We got in a huge fight last night. I told him we should take a break and that we shouldn't live together. He agreed. Except not in an amicable way. He was pissed when he left last night. He didn't come home. Looks like he waited for me to leave for class before moving his shit out and..."

"And what?" I prodded.

"He quit the team," Max said in a shaky voice.

"Why?"

"Why do you think? Are you listening? He wants to come out. He didn't think he could be out and be on the baseball team."

A suffocating silence filtered through the line.

"What are you not saying?"

"Be careful. He wants revenge. It might just be me he's after, but watch your back."

"Fuck." I swiped my hand across my jaw and nodded absently at a few of my teammates as they made their way to the lockers. "All right. Are you okay?"

Max huffed humorlessly. "Peachy. I don't know if I should talk to my coach or wait to see what Sky does, but...I'll be fine. I'm sorry, Chrissy."

"Me too. It'll be okay," I said, hoping the tired platitude was the truth before disconnecting the call.

I took a deep breath as I stuffed my cell into my bag; then I stepped onto the pathway and immediately bumped into Jonesie and Moreno. Great. I wasn't sure what to say to Jonesie after my accidental revelation Saturday night, but I wasn't engaging in a heart-to-heart with Moreno there, and I was too shaken by Max's bombshell. So I tilted my chin in greeting and headed for the locker room.

"Rafferty, wait up," Jonesie shouted.

I stopped in my tracks, frowning in response to Moreno's unfriendly scowl as he continued ahead of us. "What's up with him?"

"He's pissed 'cause you keep calling him out for being a lazy shit."

"Well, every time he's lazy, I end up splattered on the field so 'scuse me if I don't feel bad," I huffed.

"Nah, you're right." Jonesie yanked on the strap of my

workout bag before I reached the door. "About the other night..."

"What about it?" I asked nonchalantly.

"I'm not gonna say anything. I don't care who you screw. You're a great quarterback and that's all that matters." He pursed his lips and gave an uncomfortable shrug before continuing. "But, you should know there are some rumors going around. I didn't think much about it 'cause there's always some asshole who's got something to say about—"

"What kind of rumors?"

"Gay rumors about you and your roommate, the baseball player. I never thought they were true, but maybe they are. I don't know and like I said, I don't care. But it's coming up again. Moreno just told me he heard something and...I thought you'd want to know."

I swallowed hard. "Right. Thanks."

"Hey, I got your back. No worries here. And don't worry about Moreno. He doesn't really believe it anyway." Jonesie patted my back reassuringly, then moved ahead of me into the locker room.

I could hardly hear the normal everyday banter over the rush of blood to my ears. I kept my head down, got ready as quickly as possible, and hurried to the field.

After an hour or so of running drills and working on my passing game, I felt more like myself again. There would always be background noise. It might be rowdy fans, screaming coaches, the lights, the elements...but once the ref blew the whistle, the game was the only thing that mattered. Thankfully, I was fully in my zone by the end of practice. My confidence was back to peak levels.

After practice, I spoke with Perez about my idea to stay on another year. He was ecstatic and very supportive.

"Good for you, man! That's great news. I'll help you with any financial aid you might need, but honestly, I think we can work out a scholarship for a year. Looks like you won't have to take statistics again either. I heard your grade has already improved. I knew Rory was good. He's helped a lot, hasn't he?"

"Definitely."

"I'm proud of you." Perez gave me a high five, then followed it up with an impromptu hug. "I'm not gonna lie, this is good for the team. Your backup just isn't ready for prime time. Let me talk to the other coaches, I want to announce this at the big game Saturday. Or maybe sooner. I could probably do a press release and—"

"Wait. I have to talk to my parents first," I said. "Give me a couple of days."

"You got it!"

He thumped my back again, then jogged off the field. Okay. This was good. No, wait. It wasn't. I still had to deal with my parents, the Max and Sky drama, and most important, I had to work on how and when to come out.

One step at a time.

* * *

THE REST of the week dragged by with one tension-filled encounter after another. As expected, my dad was furious at the notion that I'd "squander my education to throw a ball around."

"It's a waste of time, a waste of talent, a waste of your life!" he screamed over dinner Tuesday evening.

"But it's my life. And I owe it to myself to try," I countered calmly.

He glared at me menacingly before turning his attention to stabbing the meatloaf on his plate. He wouldn't talk to me at all after that. Politics, weather, current events around town...nothing. I gave up and tried not to be bothered that every bite tasted like sawdust. I barely made it home before I vomited. I heaved over the toilet bowl with sweat dripping down my face, then sat back on my heels and wiped my brow. *Fuck me.* How was I going to tackle coming out if I couldn't even discuss my education without getting physically ill?

On top of that, Max was a wreck about his breakup with Sky. He was relieved he'd done it, but waiting for the proverbial other shoe to drop made him nervous. Hell, it made me nervous too. I tried to be supportive, but I couldn't help thinking that doing nothing was worse.

"Max, why don't you just talk to him? This isn't healthy. You haven't left the apartment in days," I chided.

"I went to the gym and class yesterday. That's all I got right now," he sighed unhappily as he clicked channels on the remote control. "Have you noticed anyone looking at you differently lately?"

"Moreno looks like he wants to kill me, but that's kinda normal. Why?"

"A girl in my psych class stared at me for two hours straight, then she cornered me afterward and told me she thought my boyfriend was super cute."

"Me or Sky?" I teased, flopping beside him on the sofa.

"Ha. Ha. I don't know and I didn't ask. I figured it was a sign I should hibernate for a while."

"I'm beginning to think we shouldn't hide."

Max muted the television and shifted to face me. "Are you saying *you* want to come out?"

"Honestly, I don't want to. Ever. Not because I'm ashamed, but because it's the least interesting thing about me. I can tell anyone who asks when I started to love football, when I wanted to play, and the day I decided I never wanted to stop playing, but I have no explanation for being gay. I don't know when it happened or why. I didn't practice. It's not a skill or a vocation.

It's just who I am. And I'm kinda tired of worrying about all the negative BS I'll have to deal with if anyone finds out. Why not just say it and get it over with?"

Max gaped at me. "Really? What about your team? Jesus, what about your parents? You said your dad lost his mind when you told him you weren't going to law school. He might actually disown you for being gay."

"But it won't make me less gay," I replied. "Same goes for my team. I can't spend my whole life hiding, Max. It feels like the longer I deny who I am, the more I let them win."

"You're really going to do it," he said in an awed tone.

"Yeah. I don't know when, but yeah...I want to. And I know we always said we were in this together but—"

"No. You have to do what's right for you."

I smiled. "Thanks. What about you?"

"I think I'll run away and join the circus or maybe move to LA and become a roadie for a famous band. The possibilities are endless," he snarked.

"Or you could be the first out baseball player drafted to the majors. You never know till you try."

Max flashed a Cheshire cat grin at me. "Rory is good for you. He doesn't look like a model for positive queer outlook, but he seems to have his shit together."

"He does. And I think it's time for me to get mine together too. Eventually. I'm not making any announcements right away, Max. I'm just mentally preparing myself for when the time seems right. Maybe after the holidays. Maybe next year. I don't know."

"I wonder how you know when the time is right. There oughtta be an app for that, so you get this *ding, ding, ding* on your phone and *boom*! You've got twenty-four hours to douse yourself in rainbow glitter and announce your homo-dom to the universe. You can choose a signature anthem and kickass wardrobe change. I'm David Bowie's Ziggy Stardust, and I'm gonna blast 'Starman.' How 'bout you?"

" 'Starman' is my favorite. Choose another."

"Since when? That's mine. You can have a Britney song," he teased.

"No fuckin' way." I tossed a throw pillow at his head, then grabbed the remote from his hand.

He pounced on top of me and in no time, we were wrestling like a couple of grade-school kids. The silly respite was a nice reminder we'd be okay. Max and I had been a team for a long time. It was time to part ways and work on our issues alone. He'd tell his story in his unique voice when he was ready, and I'd do the same. Maybe someday we'd look back at our younger selves and wonder why we'd been so afraid. Maybe ten years from now, he'd be a famous baseball player and I'd be a sought-after NFL coach. No one would talk about our sexuality; they'd be too busy celebrating our achievements. It was a good dream. But with a little blood, sweat, and tears, anything could happen.

PEREZ WANTED to announce my plans to stay on before the last game of our season that Saturday. I agreed with the timing. I'd already talked to my parents and though they weren't happy with my decision initially, my dad called me a couple of days later and said it wasn't a bad idea. He suggested I might be a bit immature for law school and that I'd benefit from another year as an undergrad. He didn't once mention football or my plans to take on a minor, but that just meant we were back to normal.

Honestly, I was relieved he was talking to me at all. It gave me one less thing to worry about before Saturday night. After we won and the announcement was made, I could think about when and how to eventually come out. Unless Sky did it for me sooner. In my quest to take an offensive approach, I decided to confront him directly. I called him several times after he left. He didn't return any of my voice messages but when I texted, he replied immediately.

Why didn't you call me back? I typed.

I don't use the phone.

Fucker. *Will you please make an exception? I need to talk to you.*

No. I growled at my cell until Sky magically added, *Text me whatever you have to say.*

I glanced up at Rory. He agreed to let our usual tutoring session slide this week and play catch with me at the park before my practice Thursday afternoon. He was dressed like me—in black workout leggings and a blue pullover that hugged his muscles and made his eyes pop.

I propped my leg on the picnic bench and refocused on the text thread. I tried to think of how to nicely ask Sky if he was about to ruin my life. Or if he'd give me the honor of doing it myself.

I settled on, *Are we cool?*

Barely but don't worry. I'm not spilling any secrets. I don't care enough to deal with your drama.

My drama? I almost asked what he meant, but I didn't want him to change his mind.

Thanks. Take care.

You're welcome. Leave me alone. Forever please.

"Ugh. He's such a little fucker. I don't get what Max saw in him," I groused before filling Rory in on the text conversation.

"You have to let it go for now," Rory commented, tossing the ball to me.

"Are you tired or can you run a couple more routes?"

"One more. We've been at this for an hour. Remind me, how is this fun again?"

I rolled my eyes and shot an indulgent smile at my

boyfriend. We hadn't used the B-word or even the L-word yet, but it was unspoken. I could feel it in the way he looked at me and I knew that in spite of his complaints, he didn't want to be anywhere else.

"It's fun because football is fun," I singsonged, launching the ball at him.

He dove for the ball and missed by an inch. His momentum sent him flying face-first onto the damp grass. I ran to his side and asked if he was okay as I brushed nonexistent dirt from his ass, then squeezed it for good measure.

Rory sprang to his feet and held his hands out for inspection. "I think we're done here."

"Poor baby." I kissed his left palm, then held his wrist still and traced the Spanish script. "You never told me what this means to you. Will you tell me now?"

He lifted one wrist and then the other. " 'In me all this fire is repeated,' and 'In me nothing is extinguished or forgotten.' Like any poem or story, you can take your own meaning and run with it, but to me, this one is about taking chances. It starts with a very practical...'I like you, but if you want me to leave, that's fine, I'm out.' But at the end, the tone changes to more of a 'If you're in this one hundred percent, I'm going to give you one hundred and ten.' It's a reminder not to give up."

"I like that. I should get a tattoo."

"What would you get?"

"I don't know. I'd have to think about it," I pronounced, hiking the ball under my arm. "Something symbolic but not clichéd. I like the writing idea too, but it would have to speak to me forever, you know?"

"You could do your jersey number or your birthday or—"

"Or I could finish that poem."

Rory stopped in his tracks and lowered his sunglasses. "I don't know the rest."

"I could look it up. Someday," I said in a lighthearted tone. "Come on. I have to get going."

He tugged at my elbow and pulled me against him, then pressed a quick kiss on my lips. "Hey, I'm...I'm—you're...you're important to me. Special. And this might be the ultimate cliché, but I want to tattoo you somewhere on my body, so I'll always remember how this feels. This day, this time. You."

"That's very...romantic," I whispered.

"Yeah, that's me. Mr. Romance. Don't tell anyone, all right?"

I walked beside him, listening to the cadence of his deep timbre above the sound of crunching leaves and birds chirping. I wished he'd parked his truck a mile away. Every footstep felt significant. I curbed my impulse to check the time so I could make a mental note because his unexpectedly lovely sentiment made me think the details mattered.

I chuckled when he grumbled good-naturedly about grass stains on his new sneakers, then gave in to temptation and glanced at my watch. Three oh five in the afternoon, November 15th. This was the day I truly fell in love with Rory.

According to my high-school football coach, every game was created equal. The first, fourth, and final games of any season should be played with the same amount of heart, grit, and intensity. Over the years, it had become my personal mantra. Sure, the championship qualifier was a big deal, but we wouldn't have come this far as a team if we hadn't worked our asses off all season. I paced the locker room like a caged tiger, pumping myself up before I called everyone into a huddle. When I had my rhythm down, I pulled my helmet over my head and signaled to Jonesie to give one of his ear-splitting whistles. Within seconds, I was surrounded by giants in full uniform. They were ready for action, but it was my job to rev them up and remind them what we were here to do.

"Whose house is this?" I yelled.

"Our house!"

"No one comes into this house to win. We gotta fight. What are we gonna do?"

"Fight, fight, fight!" they chanted in unison.

The walls shook and the locker doors rattled with the frenetic energy. I scanned my men with a note of satisfaction.

Everyone in this room loved this as much as I did. I was proud to lead them into battle. Maybe that sounded overly dramatic, but this brotherhood was found on allegiance to each other and to something bigger than ourselves. If we fought together, we'd win together. Every time.

I stopped short at the lone figure standing in the back. He was suited up in full gear like everyone else, but he remained stubbornly silent. I held his gaze for a half second, then pumped my fist in the air and gave one last rally cry before leading the charge through the tunnel and onto the field.

The crowd went wild. Our stadium was small by anyone's standards, but our games were generally well attended, and I could tell every seat in the house was spoken for tonight. Fuck, I was so damn glad I'd told Perez I wanted another season. I wasn't ready to give this up. Just being here was electrifying, but knowing a large part of the frenzy had something to do with me was indescribable.

Everyone I knew was here tonight. My family, my friends... my boyfriend. I looked up at the home side bleachers, but there was no way to spot Rory at a glance. That was okay. Just knowing he was there was enough. I made an impromptu peace sign. If he was watching me now, at least he'd know I was thinking of him.

I jogged over to the sideline for a pre-game powwow with Perez and Flannigan when they flagged me over. Flannigan reminded me of an older version of Perez. He was a big barrel-chested man in his early sixties with a thick shock of white hair. Unlike Perez, he rarely smiled. He knew a fuckton about football, though. He'd played defensive tackle forty years ago in the pros and loved to debate the integrity of any defense strategy.

I caught the football my backup tossed and nodded while Perez went over our initial play calls.

"You ready?"

"Yes, sir."

He chuckled at my formal tone. "Good. Hey, we're going to announce your plans to stay on after the game in the locker room. We invited a local paper to cover it as an exclusive story, but we'll save the press conference for after the championship game."

"Press conference? Since when are we doing press conferences?" I asked with a laugh.

"Since you ended up being one of our top winning quarterbacks, that's since when," Flannigan replied gruffly. "I don't know who'll come, but we've invited the big guns to that game... LA Times, USA Today. We'll deal with that when the time comes. Let's concentrate on winning this one. I'm moving Jonesie to cover Butterworth so Moreno will take over for—"

"No."

"Excuse me?" Flannigan glowered.

"Sorry, sir. But Moreno's head isn't in it. I think he's pissed I called him out in practice again and—"

"All right. Jonesie stays. Sanchez will take over for Butterworth," Coach said before stepping aside.

"What about Moreno?" Perez asked with a frown.

"Bench him until we need him." Flannigan smacked his hand on his clipboard and fixed us both with a hard stare. "Let's win this fucking game."

And we did.

The final score was thirty-five to six. We dominated our opponent in every way possible. My arm was strong, my receivers were sure-footed and fast, and our defense was on fire. I didn't think the stadium had ever been quite so loud. Our fans cheered wildly for us as we celebrated on the field, jumping and hooting on the sidelines. Jonesie and Sanchez hefted me onto their shoulders and carried me back through the tunnel into the locker room.

Cameras flashed as we drew closer but the noise level faded to an almost ghostly quiet. My ears were still ringing from the chaotic atmosphere on the field as we triumphantly charged the locker room. If I wasn't so high from our win, I might have noticed the silence sooner. Or the panicky glances my team-mates shot my way when Jonesie and Sanchez set me on my feet.

"What's wrong with you guys? We just won the—holy shit." I dropped my helmet on the nearest bench and stared at the graf-fiti spray painted on my locker door.

Faggot, Butt Prate, Cock Sucker...I cocked my head to study the sideways script. He misspelled pirate, I mused numbly.

"Who the fuck did this?" Jonesie roared. "I want a fuckin' answer! Now!"

I heard him as if through a vacuum. The buzzing in my head seemed to worsen in the growing silence. The eerie calm before a storm. I reached out to touch the wet paint. It was a Pepto Bismol pink. Ugly color. I'd thought I was ambivalent about colors. But now I hated pink. Or maybe I hated the quiet. It was suddenly louder than the buzzing. I had to say something. They were waiting for me to speak up. I was their leader. If this was our house, I was the king. Not really, but...sort of. I swallowed around the grapefruit in my throat and slowly turned to face my teammates. I was met with wide-eyed gazes and a barrage of panicky questions.

"Do you think it was someone on the other team? I don't see how they could have gotten in without security seeing them."

"It had to be an inside job."

"None of us would do this. We love you, man."

"Someone needs to call the police," an older voice said from the back of the room. "And get your coach in here too."

The reporter. Great. Wow. I didn't quite know how to quantify just how big of a shit show I'd walked into, but I knew it was epic. My friends and teammates, my coaches, *and* a reporter. Everyone wanted to point fingers right now or pledge their allegiance. But soon they'd start asking the obvious...why? Then would come the inevitable, "Is it true?" Let's face it, this had the earmark of a crime of passion. It was personal. Only my locker was desecrated. Whoever did it was pissed at me. They wanted to bring me down and expose me as publicly as possible. I'd bet anything it was Moreno, but I didn't have proof. What I did have was twenty-plus burly men waiting for my reaction.

I opened my mouth and closed it twice. I sucked in air like a fish on dry land and tried again.

"This is um...graphic. I guess that's the right word. I think this is a bigger reflection of whoever did this than it is of me, but—"

"Exactly. We know you're not gay, dude," one of my fullbacks said. I couldn't recall his name at the moment. Greg or Gray.

I sucked in another breath and noted Jonesie standing close by, like a sentry. The smallest tilt of his head communicated unflagging support. I curled my lips in a wan smile before addressing my nervous audience.

"Here's the thing....I am gay." Silence. Okay, fuck. I couldn't do quiet right now. I had to keep talking. I swallowed hard and continued. "I've been thinking about how to come out for a couple of weeks, but...this wasn't what I had in mind. I haven't told my parents or my sister yet. I haven't told Perez or Flannigan or any of the other coaches or professors. And I didn't tell any of you. I could say it's because I was waiting for the right time, but the truth is, I didn't know how to say it at all. To anyone. I hoped it wouldn't matter because you already know the real me. The only thing you didn't know is that I'm gay. It's like realizing your neighbor has blue eyes for the first time. He can see the same whether or not you acknowledge his eye color. Does that make sense? Maybe not."

I swiped my hand through my hair in a mixture of frustration and defeat. "Look...tonight was supposed to be about winning. We won and I'm proud of our achievement. We've had a great year. In fact, it's been a great four years for me. I don't use this phrase lightly, but I mean it when I tell you I'm *blessed* to be part of this team. You've been my family...my brothers for a long time. You've supported me on my off days, put up with my bullshit, and made me dig deeper when I thought I couldn't go on. I'd like to think I've done the same for you. I was going to announce that I'd like to stay on for a fifth year but now, this might be awkward timing," I said with a humorless half laugh before continuing. "I'm not sure how it'll work, so I'll say good-bye for now. Regardless of what happens, thank you. Thank you for being part of the best four years of my life."

Silence.

I breathed it in as I turned to open my locker. Then I pulled out my workout bag, bowed my head, and walked out.

A muffled cheer erupted and someone chanted my name, but I didn't stop. I rounded the corner and hurried to the parking lot with my head down. I didn't want to gauge the levels of support I might have. I knew too well that it was easy to offer platitudes in crowded rooms.

The fluctuation of an adrenaline high to a serious low was like being drop-kicked from a twenty-story building. My hands shook as I yanked my jersey over my head. I didn't want anyone to notice me now. I desperately needed space and anonymity...in whatever form was available.

I DIDN'T BOTHER CHECKING my messages until I was home. I showered and dressed in a pair of black sweats and an old college T-shirt and was just about to lie on the sofa and lose myself in video games when someone banged on my door.

"Christian! Open the fucking door!"

Shit.

I ran to unlatch the lock, shocked to find Rory standing there. He'd never been to my apartment. We'd always met at his place because he lived alone, and it was the perfect way to avoid the Max-and-Sky drama.

"Shh! You're going to—"

Rory swept me into his arms and kicked the door shut behind him. He held me for a while; then he pulled back slightly and captured my face. "Fuck, I was worried about you. It was complete bedlam around the locker rooms. The police descended, evacuated and cordoned off the area. Some woman I think might be your mom was crying and...what the hell happened?"

"I came out."

"And they sent a SWAT team? I don't think so. Try again."

Unbelievably, I laughed. I padded back to the sofa and typed a quick message to my mom to let her know I was okay before tossing my cell onto the coffee table and curling into a corner with a pillow clutched against my chest.

"Want something to drink?" I offered.

"No, thanks. I want you to talk to me." He cast his eyes around the open living area. "Nice place, by the way."

"Thanks. How'd you know where I live?"

"Max. I met him in the bleachers tonight. I was waiting for you to return my text, and we started talking just as all hell broke loose. I'm surprised you got out of there without anyone seeing you."

"I'm pretty quick." I shrugged weakly.

Rory flopped beside me on the sofa, snatched the pillow

from my hands, and tucked me against his chest. "I know you are."

I felt my muscles relax as he cradled my head and absently pressed kisses on my temple. He was a buoy in a storm. Literally. My cell phone vibrated noisily on the wood table, reminding me I had a slew of people who wanted answers. I supposed Rory did too, but unlike my parents, coaches, and teammates, he felt safe. For now.

I sat up slowly and told him what happened. The celebration, the graffiti, the silence, my exit speech. Everything. "I didn't know how to handle it, but I didn't want to deal with everyone, including the police, at the same time. So I said good-bye and left. Maybe leaving was cowardly, but...I couldn't face everyone."

Rory lifted my chin tenderly. "I get it. But you haven't done anything wrong."

"I know. But I couldn't deal with all that disappointment at once. My parents are super conservative and religious, Rory. They don't want to know I'm gay. Even if they suspected I was gay, they're the type of people who'd prefer not to talk about it. Ever. Did you know a reporter was in the locker room taking video? This is going to be everywhere, and there's a good chance my folks will never talk to me again. Then there's Flannigan and Perez. Their quarterback is gay. Quarterback. Not the kicker or the special-teams guy who rarely sees playing time. I'm the leader. I can't be gay. I can't—"

"Stop it. You *are* gay. And you're a good man and a strong leader. Gay isn't synonymous with weak, Christian. You know better than that," he replied firmly.

I nodded. "Yeah, but I have to convince them. I've been trying my whole life but it's not enough. I get good grades, but I suck at math. I'm a good quarterback, but I can only take it so far. Then what? I'm the gay son. The gay former athlete. I don't know what comes next. I never did. I figured I'd graduate, move and start over where no one knows me, and I don't have to worry about all the ways I'm never gonna be enough." I swiped at my face as my fears gained momentum, leaving me feeling sick and dizzy.

"Hey, that's not true. You had a crappy night and—"

"No. I had an amazing night." I jumped to my feet and paced to the window before turning to face him. "I was a fucking god out there. I had a great game. Five passing touchdowns, Rory. Five. Most pros don't do that in a single game. Sure, the competition wasn't great, but we were still on fire. Do you have any idea how it feels to go from hero to having your entire team stare at you with pity and disgust and—"

"No one was disgusted. You're projecting that. Those guys love you, Christian. I heard them after the cops came. They rallied around you. They support you. They've got your back. Do you realize how lucky you are?"

I hung my head in defeat and perched on a corner of the sofa. "In some ways, I know I am. But the rest...my parents, the coaches, my future...I don't know where to start. Fuck, I wanna run away."

"It wouldn't help. You'd still be you. And if you ask me, that's something to be proud of." Rory furrowed his brow and gave me an intense look. "I know you feel overwhelmed right now, but you're not alone. I'm here and—"

"But you can't be," I choked.

He drew back and cocked his head. "What do you mean?"

"Perez hired you. You're employed by the football program. Get it?"

"No."

"Tutor and student. Look, I'm not a celebrity and I know it, but that reporter in the locker room was supposed to cover my return next year. It was going to be a big press moment for the school and...well, it didn't go according to plan. I've been sitting here trying to figure out what'll happen next. Police investigation, school investigation, and somewhere in all this I have to think about my parents. This is how they're finding out I'm gay. Not cool. To a couple of straight-laced conservatives, this is a scandal. And my dad works for the administration. This is a shit show in the making."

"Okay. When you put it like that, it sounds bad but I'm here and—"

"No. You'll lose your job, Rory. They'll want a story about the guy who works at the YMCA. They'll drag you into a story that isn't yours and tell lies and make us seem...dirty."

Rory huffed belligerently. "I can handle it."

"I can't."

An eerie silence crept from every corner of the room. It was oppressive and bleak, covering me like a heavy blanket in summertime. I wanted to kick it off, open a window, and undo the day. But couldn't help wondering if I'd brought this on myself. All I knew was, I couldn't bring him down with me.

"What does that mean?" he asked.

I pursed my lips, hoping to keep the flood of emotion at bay when I spoke again. "We have to go our own way. For now. Maybe, I can fix this and we can be together someday, but...not now."

Rory went still. He didn't move or breathe for a long, painful minute. Finally, his nostrils flared and his hands trembled. He flattened them on his thighs as if to stop the shaking. When it didn't work, he stood and paced to the opposite side of the coffee table.

"I don't want to go."

"You have to. I don't want to hurt you. I don't want to drag you through this mess," I whispered unhappily.

"Baby, I get that this isn't easy. I get that it isn't what you planned. I'm sorry some asshole took a shot at you, and I'm sorry you're hurting. It fucking kills me." His voice hitched with pain. He paused for a moment before continuing. "But I want to tell you something. Being with you isn't a crime. We're good and we're right. We're exactly who we're supposed to be and—"

"Rory."

"No, let me finish. You are by far, the best thing that's ever happened to me. I couldn't believe my luck when I first met you, and I realized you were smart and funny and just a little dopey at math. I don't know how this happened so fast, but I'm in over my head now. I want to slay all those fucking dragons and make things right. I don't know what to do or what to say to make this better. But I want you to know that I'm here." He reached for my hands and squeezed them tightly. "And I love you."

I opened my mouth and stared at him in shock. "Love."

"Yeah, love. I said it. Look, I swear I'm not trying to make this complicated. I'm not asking anything from you. I know you think you gotta do this by yourself, but maybe it'll help to know that you're not alone. Not really." His voice was raw with emotion when he continued. "There's always someone thinking about you."

"Rory, I'm..."

He pulled me into a fierce embrace and held me close. Then he let go and moved to the door. "Go do your thing. If you need me, I'll come. Day or night, call me. We can meet at Starbucks or throw a football in the park. Whatever. I can be flexible...I just— I don't want to lose you, so if we can—"

"You're not gonna lose me. I promise," I choked, launching myself at him and holding on for dear life.

Rory ran soothing fingers through my hair while I sobbed big, ugly tears. When I finally calmed down, he kissed my forehead and gently pushed me away. He gave me one last longing look before opening the door and stepping into the hallway.

I closed my eyes as the lock clicked shut and braced my hand on the wall to keep myself upright. Everything in me ached. My bones, my muscles, my mind. I'd left part of my heart and soul on the football field, but the biggest part of me just walked out the door. I had nothing left. I was empty. Nothing inside me and nothing left to give. Nothing.

JUST AS I EXPECTED, all hell broke loose.

The reporter's video clip of me coming out to my team in front of my vandalized locker was trending on social media. By Sunday afternoon, I'd become an unwitting sensation. I was a poster boy for LGBTQ athletes or an immoral sinner, depending upon whom you asked. I was followed to the gym and back, and again later that evening when I sucked up the nerve to visit my parents for our traditional Sunday night dinner. My father pulled back the curtain in the living room, then cast a disproving look between me and the photographer leaning outside the passenger side of a black Suburban. But he didn't say a word.

My mom made idle conversation about the state of her mashed potatoes and a new recipe she wanted to try for the holidays. I didn't know how to respond. If my presence was barely tolerated during a simple dinner, I doubted I'd be welcome during the holidays. After a while, she gave up. We sat in an uncomfortable triangle of silence until I finally said good-bye.

Which of course, was when my father decided to speak up. "I'll see you at the meeting tomorrow."

"What meeting?"

"Administration has called a meeting with the athletic department to discuss what occurred yesterday. The detective assigned to the case may also be in attendance. I don't know," he said coolly.

"Detective?"

"Yes. They're launching an investigation. If you know who did this, you should speak up and save the taxpayers some money. Was it a...lover?"

I didn't think I'd ever heard anyone make a pleasant five-letter word sound like a vile four-letter one. I narrowed my gaze and let out a humorless huff.

"No. Thanks for asking," I said sarcastically.

"Don't take a tone with me, boy. Do you have any idea what you've done to this family?" he spat.

I studied the vein in his temple and marveled that it didn't pop. "Yeah, I know what I've done. I also know what I haven't done."

My father glared at me with his fists clenched. "You have ruined our name! You've brought shame and disgrace to all of us. You didn't have the common courtesy to deny those accusations. You didn't stop to think of anyone but yourself."

"I can't listen to this. I won't take on your guilt or shame. I'm proud of who I am," I insisted.

"How can you be?" He shook his head angrily. "I don't want to talk about this. There's nothing more to say. That meeting is your opportunity to clear our name. I expect you to do it, boy."

"I'm not a boy. I'm a man. And I have nothing to hide." I paused on the threshold and gave my mother a nod I hoped passed for a civil good-bye before meeting my father's gaze. "See ya tomorrow...Dad."

MAX TOOK one look at me when I got home that night and made a giant pot of homemade hot cocoa. It was some special recipe with ancho chili that was supposed to enhance the chocolate flavor. I loved it. His mom used to make extra when I came over. And when we first moved in together, Max made it whenever he knew I'd had a crap day. He handed me a large mug, set a blanket over my legs, and passed me one of the X-Box game controllers. Unlike the oppressive silence at my parents' house, this was nice. I could breathe here.

"I'm sorry, Chrissy. I'm sorry about Sky and—"

"Sky didn't do it."

"No, I didn't think so. Not his style. But that's not what I meant." He bit his lips and set his controller aside, then shifted to face me on the sofa. "I'm sorry I let him in. I'm sorry it ended what we had. We were good together and—"

"No. We were kids, Max. We were never going to make it in the long run. We both know it. If it wasn't Sky, it would have been someone or something else."

"Maybe." He waited a beat and asked, "Do you want me to go with you tomorrow? For moral support?"

"Thanks, but no."

"What about Rory? He'd be there in a heartbeat."

I shook my head slowly. "Yeah, but...I need to do this alone. And when you come out, it'll be the same for you."

"I'm gonna order a little less drama when I make my rainbow announcement," he joked.

"Hey, do it when you're ready, and do it on your terms."

Max frowned. "This wasn't on your terms. This was fucked!"

"Yeah, I know. And I've been sitting here feeling sorry for myself thinking how unfair this shit is, but I think I'm doing this wrong. I need to play offense."

"Huh?"

"Nothing. Just thinking out loud." I picked up my controller and gestured for him to do the same. "Let's do this. I'm ready to kick some ass."

PEREZ LEFT me multiple messages over the weekend pledging his support. He reiterated it when we talked briefly Monday morning, but I knew his personal support didn't necessarily translate to retaining my spot on the team next year. There were many more factors at play, and unfortunately neither Flannigan or Perez had a final say in the matter. Chilton was a private university. I knew the second I walked into that stuffy conference room with a handful of men in suits that my fate might have been decided before I even opened my mouth.

And forty minutes later, I was sure of it.

"Given the nature of this case...the vandalism to school property and the police investigating the matter as a possible hate crime, the board feels it would be prudent to advise the athletic department to withdraw consideration for Mr. Rafferty to continue as a fifth-year quarterback in the hopes that this will allow law enforcement to punish the responsible party and bring justice to the Rafferty family. It would also—"

"Bullshit," I exclaimed, jumping to my feet.

"Christian!" My father hissed.

"No. This is wrong. I'd like to take the opportunity to remind you all of a few things. I didn't commit a crime. A crime was committed against me, an LGBTQ member of your student body. I am responsible for four winning seasons that have resulted in three championship wins during my tenure as a student athlete here. I've gone above and beyond my duties as quarterback to ensure I've represented Chilton with honor, pride, and respect. So I'm sorry...you'll have to excuse me if I don't quite comprehend the supposed justice behind removing me from my position. I'm the best thing you've got going at the moment. You can hide behind your rhetoric of propriety and community standards, or you can wake up and take a look around you. I am a voice for this community...as an athlete, a student, and a leader. If you choose not to stand behind me, you stand against me and every minority at this school. Make no mistake, this was a hate crime. Deal with it responsibly. Don't back down."

I took a cleansing breath and looked around the oval conference table at the shocked expressions of the board members. Well, not everyone was shocked. My father looked apoplectic. But when I glanced over at my coaches and caught the reluctant humor on Flannigan's lips and Perez's huge shit-eating grin, I felt oddly vindicated. *Fuck the rest of them.* I loved football, I loved my time at this school, but I wouldn't let someone else's act of cowardice define my legacy as an athlete or a person. I was better than this. And I had much more to give.

"If you have any further questions, have your people talk to my people," I said, gesturing to my coaches. "Please excuse me, gentlemen. I have a statistics test to study for. Thanks for your time."

My father called my name, but I didn't look back. I had nothing more to say, and I definitely wouldn't apologize.

I raced out of the administration building and typed a quick message on my cell as I made my way across campus. It was a gorgeous day. The sun was shining, but it was cool and crisp, like a good autumn day should be. A few students gave me high fives and fist bumps. A few others shouted, "We love you, Christian!" or some variation of "You're cool, man," as I headed for my car.

I wasn't cool or special, but I had my moments. I needed one more major moment today 'cause at the end of the day, I didn't care about my place on the team or in my family. My future happiness depended on something and someone else entirely, and I was going to do whatever I could to get it back.

Twenty minutes later, I pulled up into the Starbucks parking lot. When I didn't see Rory's truck in the lot, my heart nosedived to my stomach. Maybe he changed his mind. I checked his text response again. *I'll be there.* Rory never said anything he didn't mean.

I checked my reflection in the window as I walked toward the entrance. I hated wearing a suit and tie. I looked like a dweeb in grown-up clothes. I hooked my finger in the knot to loosen it, pushed the door open, and headed for the counter. I placed my order before stepping aside to wait with my gaze trained on the door. Funny enough, I felt his presence before I saw him. I turned to thank the barista for my drinks, then looked up and there he was.

And just like that, everything fell into place.

I met Rory at our table by the window and set the cups down before taking a seat.

"What the hell is that?"

"A pumpkin spice latte," I replied, biting my lower lip.

"I hate that shit."

"It's not yours, it's mine."

"You always get iced coffee. Something's up with you," he said suspiciously. "You look hot, by the way. Can I say that, or is that against tutor-student rules?"

"You can say it," I replied with a smile.

He returned my smile with a weaker version, then tapped his fingers on the table. "Where's your book?"

"I didn't bring it. I just wanted to talk to you. I kind of panicked and this seemed like a good place and—"

"Is everything okay?"

"No."

Rory furrowed his brow. "What happened? Did they kick you off the team or out of school? They can't do that, you know."

"Huh? No," I replied, waving dismissively. "I wasn't talking about football or school. That's not important."

"Then what—"

"I love you," I blurted.

"I—"

"No. Please, let me talk. Everything around me is crashing and burning. I have to wait till the smoke clears to see what's left, but to be honest...I don't really care. Yeah, I'll be sad if my football career is over, but it's gonna end someday anyway. And I'm trying to come to grips with the idea that my family life as I knew it is over. I can't change myself to make my parents happy. This is who I am. And I think I'm gonna be okay. But I'll be a million times better with you."

"Christ—"

"Wait. Let me say everything. You told me you'd fight for me. You said you'd stand by me. I knew I had to work through the BS on my own. So I stood up in front of a bunch of old guys in suits and I thought to myself, 'What would Rory do?' And you know what? I kicked ass and I have no regrets. You're my rock, my teacher, my friend. I want to be that for you too. For the rest of our lives. I don't care where we live, what we do...I just want you."

Rory stood and pulled me into his arms. We held each other in a strong embrace until he pushed back slightly to seal his lips over mine. The kiss was sweet and full of promise. It marked a beginning of sorts. Our beginning.

We broke for air and grinned at each other like a couple of fools.

"I love you. You've always been stronger than you think, baby."

"Maybe so."

"Hmm. But you still have to pass statistics," he teased.

I threw my head back and laughed before wrapping my arms around his neck.

I didn't stop to wonder what we looked like to the average passerby. Two men engaged in a passionate embrace in a coffee shop in broad daylight. One dressed in a suit and tie and the other in casual jeans and a jacket that covered his ink. If anyone was offended by our public display, they didn't say a word. Not that I cared. I was done hiding, and I was done worrying about what others thought. This man and the life we made were all that mattered. It was time to set my old worries aside, come out on the offense, and begin anew.

EPILOGUE

"You must allow me to tell you how ardently I admire and love you."—Jane Austen, *Pride and Prejudice*

THE PET STORE seemed more crowded than usual for a Thursday evening. Then again, everywhere in Long Beach was somewhat congested in summertime. School was out and tourist season was in full swing. It made sense that parking spaces were harder to come by near the beach in June, but I certainly didn't think we'd be brushing elbows with the masses to get to the cat corner.

We passed a gaggle of kids jumping excitedly in front of the lizard and snake displays and another group pointing at the exotic fish aquarium before stopping to check out a few toys along the way.

"Buttons needs this," I said, holding up a hot dog in a bun squeeze-toy.

Rory rolled his eyes. "That's for dogs, not cats. The queen wouldn't be impressed."

"Then I think we should get a dog. A small, hypoallergenic one. No shedding, no fuss, no mess. What do you say?"

"We aren't home enough. You've got to walk a dog, play with a dog, and be around in general. Cats are easy. They just want to be left alone. The more you play with Buttons, the more she thinks you're a psycho to be avoided at all costs. See? Much easier."

"Ha. Maybe I'm the needy one. You have to admit that it would be nice to have a little canine friend around, though. We have a yard now. We can do it!"

Rory and I moved into a cute two-bedroom bungalow a couple of blocks from the ocean. It was just two miles from Rory's old apartment, but it was a million times nicer. The bathroom and kitchen needed updating, but it had cool original features like hardwood flooring and arched doorways. Best of all, it had a yard that was big enough to host friends and certainly enough room for a puppy to romp around.

But Rory was right. Our schedules were erratic. Between classes and training clients at the YMCA and substitute teaching, he was busier than ever. And in the fall, he'd be back in school himself, working toward his master's degree. He'd been accepted into an elite program at UCLA, and while he wasn't thrilled to take on student-loan debt, he knew the degree was necessary if he wanted to become a mathematics professor. The idea alone of my hunky man pointing out complicated equations on a chalkboard with his sleeves rolled up, exposing his tattoos and accentuating his muscles, made me swoon. None of my college professors had ever looked like him. I might have been more interested if I'd had eye-candy incentive. Now I was just happy I never had to take another math class again.

Thankfully, I passed both semesters of statistics, so I could concentrate on my minor when I returned for my fifth and final year at Chilton. I signed up for two summer classes that began the end of June, but I had a little more free time than normal. Of course, that wouldn't be the case in August when football season was in full swing again.

The board issued a private apology to me and publicly offered me a scholarship for my final year. And yes, I was starting quarterback. The difference this time was that I had an idea of what I wanted to do with my life. Or at least I had a path and some general direction. It could take years, but I might just make it to the NFL one day after all. To be play caller for an elite organization would truly be part of a dream come true.

I already had the other part of that dream. I was out. Fully and completely and very proudly out of the closet. And the crazy thing was that others wanted to hear my story. I'd been interviewed and asked to speak for various LGBTQ organizations to give my perspective on being a gay athlete. For someone who'd been buried in a dark closet for years, it was life-changing. I couldn't imagine talking freely about my boyfriend or our life together even nine months ago. Now, I couldn't shut up.

Sure, it bothered me sometimes that my parents distanced themselves from me. My sister tried to be supportive, and my mom checked in with an occasional phone call or text, but my father had gone radio silent. For the first time ever, I spent the holidays elsewhere. I thought I would have been more shaken, but honestly, I expected it. I was never going to be what my dad wanted. He hoped for a version of himself, and a gay son wasn't it. But that was his problem, not mine. I had friendship, joy, and more love in my life than I'd ever imagined. I wouldn't give up a moment of it just to make him more comfortable. That wasn't love. I knew the difference now.

"Like I said, Buttons wouldn't approve. C'mon, let's check out the cat crap," Rory said, slipping his hand in mine.

I chuckled at his playful gruff intonation and let him lead the way to a ginormous array of cat scratching posts. I bypassed the humble traditional posts and marched straight for the one that looked like a cross between a jungle gym and a mini palace. It was a series of boxes with steps and tethered balls and a private box, ideal for ignoring humans.

"This one," I declared decisively. "It's perfect."

"It's huge," he deadpanned, pointing at a small version, with fewer balls and stairs. "What about that one?"

"Hmm. Kinda boring. This is a castle, that's a...condo."

"Cats dig condos. And if you think about it, she likes small spaces. Too much room might intimidate her," he reasoned patiently.

"Maybe you're right. Besides, we'll need a place for the dog bed later," I singsonged.

"Drip, drip, drip..."

"What's that supposed to mean?"

"You're torturing me till you get your way. I'm on to you. You think if you say dog once a day between now and Thanksgiving, you'll get a puppy for Christmas."

I furrowed my brow in annoyance. "Will it work?"

"Probably," Rory admitted. "I love you, baby. I'd give you anything you wanted if I could. A dog, a cat, a cow, a winning lottery ticket, a private tropical island...you name it and I promise I'll do whatever it takes to make it happen. The cow might be tricky. Not sure where we'd put it. And the lottery ticket might be a two-dollar scratcher but—"

I set my hand over his mouth and removed it quickly to seal my lips over his. I could have sworn I saw stars when I finally pulled away. "All I want is you."

"No cow?"

I shook my head and grinned so wide my face hurt. "No. Just you. I love you too. Let's get the small one."

"That's the spirit." Rory nipped my chin playfully, then whispered in my ear. "I'll give you something big when we get home, QB."

I snickered at his juvenile comeback and kissed his cheek. "I can't wait."

And why wait anyway? Patience might be a virtue, but I'd learned it was equally important to know when to act, to seize opportunity and use my voice. I'd come out on the offense...and with this man by my side, I was truly free.

STARTING AT ZERO - COMING SPRING 2019

EXCERPT FROM STARTING AT ZERO BY LANE HAYES (SPRING 2019)

"Hang on. I have one more thing to add." Gray closed the distance between us and gave me a thorough once over before continuing. "Whatever ideas Charlie put in your head about me...forget it. I'm not interested."

I furrowed my brow. "You know about the band idea?"

He rolled his eyes. "It's an ongoing thing for Char. He's been on a mad quest to rule the world since he was five. And I think he'll actually do it one day. But I doubt you're his ticket to stardom."

I should have laughed it off 'cause I one thousand percent agreed with him. However, I didn't like the notion I'd been sized up and discarded by someone who didn't know anything about me. No one should be judged on "Sweet Caroline", for fuck's sake.

"Oh really? Why not?" I deadpanned.

He stared at me for a long moment as though willing me to back down and maybe even change the subject. Silence. Finally, he leaned against the wall and crossed his arms.

"You're a good looking guy, Justin. You're young and if you're hungry enough, you can make things happen for yourself. I'm not trying to be a dick, but if playing music is where your heart lies, you need to hone your skills. You're a beginner. That's not a bad thing, but there are a million good guitarists who think their band is the next big deal. The ones who make it aren't always the best musicians, but they're almost always the bravest. I don't think you have what it takes...yet."

I was too taken aback to say anything at first. When I finally found my voice, all I say was, "Fuck you."

"And that's the other thing." He pushed away from the wall and stepped into my space until we stood toe to toe. "I'm not gonna fuck you."

My forehead creased hard enough to give me a headache. "Excuse me? Are you for real?"

"I am. Don't look so insulted. Hey, it's smart business to lay it all out before you get started. I'd hate for you to have any false expectations. If you think taking this job is gonna get you some kind of special treatment or help further your career aspirations, think again."

I shook my head in a sort of daze. Fuck him. Like big time, fuck, fuck, fuck him. And fuck Charlie. I should have known this was too good to be true. I figured I'd be the one to say or do something stupid though. Not Gray. I was the last person who'd ever seduce someone to get ahead. According to the shit storm I'd unleashed a few months ago, I had the opposite problem. I'd followed my instincts with the help of tequila and ended up getting caught in a compromising situation with my pants around my ankles and my dick up someone's ass. I was an expert at destroying opportunity, not exploiting it.

There had to be twenty perfect comeback lines, but I couldn't think of one. Nothing funny, nothing snarky, and certainly nothing intelligent. Surprise warred with pride and made it difficult for me to see through the fiery red haze clouding my vision, let alone think of a pleasant way to tell him to take the generous salary, all the perks, and his ginormous record collection and shove them up his ass. And when he stared at me as if waiting for polite reassurance or an apology of some kind, I did what I always did when I got pissed and frustrated...AKA, the opposite of what I should have done.

I pushed Gray's chest and backed him against the wall, then I captured his face between my hands and sealed my mouth over his in a rough kiss. My non-violent version of a 'fuck you'.

It didn't go quite as planned. I was a novice when it came to unleashing my bi side. I mistakenly thought I could feign indifference to things I was just beginning to realize turned me on. I forgot how much I loved the scrape of a beard against my face. And I forgot how satisfying it felt to hover over a masculine man and know for half a second, he wasn't entirely immune to me. His lips were soft, his breath was warm and I could have sworn his dick was getting hard. Or was that just me?

Gray gaped at me in shock when I broke the connection and stepped back. He set his fingers over his lips and narrowed his eyes. "Why did you do that?"

"'Cause you told me not to."

ABOUT THE AUTHOR

Lane Hayes is grateful to finally be doing what she loves best. Writing full-time! It's no secret Lane loves a good romance novel. An avid reader from an early age, she has always been drawn to well-told love story with beautifully written characters. These days she prefers the leading roles to both be men. Lane discovered the M/M genre a few years ago and was instantly hooked. Her debut novel was a 2013 Rainbow Award finalist and subsequent books have received Honorable Mentions, and were First Place winners in the 2016 and 2017 Rainbow Awards. She loves red wine, chocolate and travel (in no particular order). Lane lives in Southern California with her amazing husband in a newly empty nest.

*Be sure to join Lane's reading group, Lane's Lovers, on Facebook for immediate updates!

www.lanehayes.wordpress.com

ALSO BY LANE HAYES

Out in the Deep
Out in the End Zone

Leaning Into Love
Leaning Into Always
Leaning Into the Fall
Leaning Into a Wish
Leaning Into Touch
Leaning Into the Look
Leaning Into Forever

A Kind of Truth
A Kind of Romance
A Kind of Honesty
A Kind of Home

Better Than Good
Better Than Chance
Better Than Friends
Better Than Safe

The Right Words
The Wrong Man
The Right Time

A Way with Words

A Way with You

Made in the USA
San Bernardino, CA
16 January 2019